THE SINGING SLEUTH

THE SINGING SLEUTH

D. B. Barton

4/8/06

To Diane
I hope my book
keeps you on the
edge of your seat.
Best Wishes
Diane Barton

iUniverse, Inc.

New York Lincoln Shanghai

THE SINGING SLEUTH

iUniverse books may be ordered through booksellers or by contacting:

iUniverse
2021 Pine Lake Road, Suite 100
Lincoln, NE 68512
www.iuniverse.com
1-800-Authors (1-800-288-4677)

ISBN-13: 978-0-595-35452-8 (pbk)
ISBN-13: 978-0-595-79945-9 (ebk)
ISBN-10: 0-595-35452-1 (pbk)
ISBN-10: 0-595-79945-0 (ebk)

Printed in the United States of America

To Ariane, my daughter,
whose death is teaching me
to place my trust in God.

C O N T E N T S

Pegasus Itinerary

Southern Dreams' Tour

Flagship Cruise Line

Regular Cruise Schedule

Day	Date	Ports of Call	Arrive	Depart
Mon	23rd Jan	Fort Lauderdale, FL		04:30 PM
Tues	24th Jan	**at sea**		
Wed	25th Jan	**at sea**		
Thur	26th Jan	St. Maarten	07:00 AM	03:00 PM
Fri	27th Jan	Barbados	11:00 AM	10:00 PM
Sat	28th Jan	Martinique	07:00 AM	02:00 PM
Sun	29th Jan	**at sea**		
Mon	30th Jan	**at sea**		
Tues	31st Jan	Coral Cay	08:00 AM	04:00 PM
Wed	1st Feb	Fort Lauderdale, FL	07:30 AM	

Reverse Cruise Schedule

Day	Date	Ports of Call	Arrive	Depart
Wed	1st Feb	Fort Lauderdale, FL		04:30 PM
Thur	2nd Feb	Coral Cay	08:00 AM	04:00 PM
Fri	3rd Feb	**at sea**		
Sat	4th Feb	**at sea**		
Sun	5th Feb	Martinique	07:00 AM	03:00 PM
Mon	6th Feb	Barbados	11:00 AM	10:00 PM
Tues	7th Feb	St. Maarten	07:00 AM	02:00 PM
Wed	8th Feb	**at sea**		
Thur	9th Feb	**at sea**		
Fri	10th Feb	Fort Lauderdale, FL	07:30 AM	

PROLOGUE

▼

Sunday Morning
22nd of January
5:10 A.M. EST

Mark's killer entered the health spa of the Pegasus. The reception area was empty and welcoming. Overstuffed chairs and couches were positioned around the room in casual seating arrangements. The carpeting was thick and luxurious, and the air was fragrant with the invigorating aromas of eucalyptus and peppermint. The environment served to heighten the executioner's sense of purpose and set the stage for a perfect murder.

The assassin believed it was a public service to slay Mark Linley. The soon-to-be-dead victim was the controller of the cruise ship. Mark's job was to make certain his coworkers pressured passengers into spending large sums of money on extra shipboard fees and services. If department managers fell short of meeting their goals, Mark Linley took great pleasure in alerting his superiors in London. Over the years, he had come to make a great many enemies.

If Mark's self righteous attitude wasn't reason enough to provoke animosity, there was also his unsettling appearance. Mark's piercing eyes stared like a dead fish on a bed of ice, his sharp nose intruded into the affairs of others, and when he pursed his thin red lips, he resembled the "Church Lady" on the old *Saturday Night Live* series. It was really surprising that the controller had managed to live so long.

While walking past the receptionist's desk, Mark's assailant entertained these thoughts. The perpetrator, however, was mostly concerned about the time. Even though the killer's wristwatch indicated it was 5:10 A.M., there was no time to dally.

From the outer room, the malefactor watched Mark. He appeared to be asleep on a large almond-shaped piece of health equipment. To be specific, the machine was called an Alpha Capsule. Its function was to relax its occupants with soothing music, perfumed herbs, heat, and massage. The top half of the apparatus was hinged to the bottom half at the foot of the device. Mark Linley's executioner was amused to see the controller's head sticking out of the capsule. He looked like a turtle trapped on his back.

It was Mark's custom to sneak into the gym early each morning to steal a few precious minutes on the machine. Being a remarkably tense person, he found it was the only place on the ship where he could unwind and collect his thoughts. Gwen, the fitness instructor, told him that twenty-five minutes in the unit were equivalent to four hours of sleep. In the last few months, Mark needed to increase his usage. He had become addicted to the capsule.

Certain that Linley was "dead to the world," the murderer walked into the huge gym. Assorted pieces of exercise equipment stood along the circumference of the glass-enclosed room like soldiers ready to do battle. In an area off to the side, a rack of neatly arranged dumbbells attracted the assassin's attention. Heading toward the weights, the assailant thought, "Soon, very soon, I'll be rid of that mealy-mouthed nuisance."

Even if the controller hadn't been asleep, he would not have heard his attacker approach. The Alpha Capsule was a loud machine. Its tiny massaging fingers made low rumbling noises, and the spray of aromatic herbs constantly swished. In addition to those sounds, Mark was listening to New Age music. High-pitched whale songs periodically screeched from the headphones.

Standing beside the rack of dumbbells, the murderer proceeded to test several weights, searching for one that had the proper mass and balance. The killer suspected that blunt force trauma to Mark's head would cause profuse bleeding and spurting. The assassin wanted to be certain that a single blow would accomplish the task.

The executioner chose a ten-pound weight for its maneuverability. Although a heavier dumbbell would cause more damage, it couldn't be wielded as swiftly or with as much accuracy as a lighter one. The ship's barbells consisted of metallic disc-like plates that screwed to the ends of four-inch rods. Unlike dumbbells made from molded rubber, these made ideal bludgeons. All telltale traces of sweat and skin could be removed easily from the shaft.

The weights that had been handled were wiped clean with a terrycloth towel that hung innocently at the end of the rack. The fitness center was well equipped to do away with the controller. Everything was within arm's reach.

The killer approached Mark. This time, the assailant's footfalls fell on the gym's low-tufted multicolor carpet. The murderer's gait was slow, yet purposeful.

Seconds later, Mark's slayer was positioned behind his head. For a moment, the killer wondered whether the controller's death was really necessary. But soon, it became utterly apparent that Mark Linley could ruin everything with one well-placed remark.

Lifting the barbell with force and precision, the executioner slammed the weight down on Mark Linley's face. One plate of the dumbbell struck him under the nose, and the other plate hit him squarely on the forehead. Blood immediately began to squirt and gush from his nostrils. The controller never stirred.

The thud of steel impacting flesh especially delighted Mark's killer. Now nothing stood in the way of the perpetrator's plans.

Holding the blood and skin encrusted barbell, the assassin walked over to the rest rooms. Right of the doors was a pop-up container of moist towelettes. The sign above it read, "For hygienic reasons, kindly wipe off equipment after use." Mark's murderer gave a sardonic laugh, wondering whether Flagship Cruise Line had ever envisioned that its cleaning supplies would be used in such a manner.

Taking several sheets from the dispenser, the assassin removed debris from the plates and fingerprints from the smooth metallic bar. The dumbbell was replaced on the rack, and the bloodstained wipes were stuffed into the killer's pockets to be disposed of later.

It was that simple.

Gazing back at the corpse, the murderer noticed rivulets of blood flowing to the floor. The dense carpeting absorbed the liquid as well as it concealed footprints. Feeling secure and confident, Mark's executioner strode to the exit.

Passing the receptionist's desk on the way out, the assailant checked the time once again and experienced a sense of immortality. It was 5:30.

Soon the fitness center would be full of activity with passengers eager to begin their morning routines. On leaving the scene of the crime, the murderer thought, "The fools on *this* ship will never know that I killed Mark Linley."

CHAPTER 1

▼

"JUST A SONG BEFORE I GO"

Words & Music—Graham Nash

Monday Morning—23rd of January

Alec DunBarton was running away from home. Home had been Scotland for the first twenty-six years of his life and England for the last sixteen. Right now, he didn't think he'd miss either.

As he fastened his seat belt, he began to feel optimistic. It was a sensation he hadn't experienced in a long time. Soon, he'd be on his way. The plane was due to leave Heathrow Airport shortly, and nine hours later, he'd be in Miami.

Last evening was a blur. Just yesterday, Douglas telephoned ship-to-shore from the Pegasus. After Douglas explained the reason for his call, it took Alec less than five minutes to accept his proposal. It was odd that a stranger's death could fill his life with purpose again.

Amidst the background noises of flight departure were newspapers rustling, overhead storage compartments being slammed, and flight attendants asking passengers to place their seats into upright positions. Alec enjoyed the sounds of travel.

Looking out the window, he wondered whether he'd adjust to living on a cruise ship again. He had been a young man when he worked on the Delphinus as an assistant controller. In those days, Alec's field of study was hotel management. After serving in the Mediterranean for eighteen months, Alec returned to college to major in banking and finance. Although it was fun to see the world, he knew he would eventually want to settle down.

With a throb of the engines, the aircraft began to taxi along the tarmac.

The plane moved past low warehouses, baggage carts, and oil trucks. Gazing at the surroundings, Alec cleared his throat and sang, "Just a song before I go, To whom it may concern. Traveling twice the speed of sound, It's easy to get burned."

"Sir, are you all right?" a concerned voice called from his left.

Alec glanced at the young woman and smiled sheepishly. "Oh sure lass, I forgot where I was for a second. I never really understood those words, but they seem to fit the moment. My name is Alec DunBarton." Extending his hand, he asked, "What's yours?"

Suddenly reticent, she shook his hand limply and whispered, "Amy. Amy Cohen."

"Well Amy, are you on your way back to the States?"

After a slight pause, she replied, "Uh, yeah. I've been on Christmas break."

Alec was about to respond when the captain announced that they'd been given clearance to take off. The plane turned onto the runway, lining up behind several other aircraft. The fight attendants took their positions in the aisles, pointed to the exits, and demonstrated the use of seatbelts, oxygen, and flotation devices.

In the meantime, Amy pulled out a huge English history textbook from her knapsack and proceeded to highlight almost every line on the page. Alec would have laughed out loud, but he had already scared the poor kid enough for one day.

It was a real blessing that no one was sitting between them. Just last night, Alec placed his airline reservation. On such short notice, he was grateful to get a seat on this flight. Alec wondered whether his luck was changing.

Suddenly the high-pitched engines roared, signaling that takeoff was imminent. He loved the way the aircraft surged forward and pulled away from the ground. It always invigorated him. The only part of flying Alec disliked was the change in air pressure. He didn't care for swallowing on demand, especially without a drink.

Glimpsing at his watch, Alec noted that the plane left on time. It was 9:50 A.M. Although it was rather early for a whisky, he knew he wouldn't say no. Whenever Alec needed to think, he would reach for his old briar pipe, stuff it thoughtfully, and draw on it until wisps of smoke circled his head. He was certain it helped him concentrate. Since smoking was prohibited on board, a drink was second best.

Alec was glad to see the flight attendant bringing the beverage cart down the aisle. Most people were ordering coffee and soft drinks. When the attendant approached him, Alec asked with a sparkle in his eyes, "Miss, do you have single-malt whisky?"

Looking through the miniature bottles, she shook her head and replied, "They may have one in first class. Let me check for you."

The flight attendant quickly returned with several bottles.

While she placed them on her trolley, she said, "We have both Glenlivet and Glenfiddich. Which one would you prefer?"

In Alec's opinion Glenfiddich was less smoky and fruitier than Glenlivet. He answered, "Why, Glenlivet, of course."

Twisting open the bottle, she asked, "Ice?"

He grinned good-naturedly and answered, "Neat, please."

Alec had been raised in Inverness. Although, he later moved to London, Alec considered himself a Scotsman through and through. No highlander would dare drink single-malt whisky diluted with ice or water. As the flight attendant passed the glass to Alec, she appeared to see him for the first time. It was a *look* he'd become increasingly familiar with over the last few years. After taking a second glance, the flight attendant continued down the passageway to the next row of seats.

Alec had the dubious distinction of resembling one of the actors who played James Bond—Pierce Brosnan. Alec had twenty pounds on that bulked-up Bond, as well as bushy eyebrows that had a will of their own, expressive brown eyes, and a broad face that was decidedly engaging. Like Brosnan, he had a full head of dark brown hair, but Alec's was graying at the temples.

Growing up, Alec had watched all of the Bond films. At times, he wished he could be as debonair and ruthless as his favorite 007: Sean Connery. Alec, though, had other qualities.

Anxious to go over the events on the Pegasus, Alec placed his drink on the tray table and searched inside his jacket for the e-mails he had received from Douglas. After he pulled them from his breast pocket, Alec took a large swallow of Glenlivet, savored the robust flavor, and read the first one.

Subj:	Murder on the Pegasus
Date:	22nd January, 4:20:06 PM EST
From:	DAbbot953@Pegasus.com
To:	AlecDunBarton@aol.com

Alec my boy,

It was wonderful to hear your voice on the phone. I wish it weren't under such bizarre circumstances. As I outlined before, we've had a rather brutal murder here. Our controller was killed this morning in the gym.

After that, all hell broke loose. Captain Jarvis and the chief of security called headquarters first, then the British Embassy, State Department, FBI, Coast Guard, and Fort Lauderdale Sheriff's Department. If it weren't so bloody awful, I would have laughed. No one could tell them who had legal jurisdiction. We were a day's journey from Port Everglades, in international waters.

The sheriff's office finally decided to take the case. Our security officer was told to photograph the body from every conceivable angle. The ME asked me to wrap Mark Linley (our victim) in plastic and put him in the morgue's cooler. His poor face was barely recognizable and covered with blood.

Although the body was discovered shortly after 6:00, some of the passengers got wind of it. We closed the gym right away and told them that the air conditioning was on the fritz. I'm sure the cruise line will be getting an earful.

As you know, our board of directors wants this matter cleared up ASAP. The captain thinks it was one of the crew. Linley was high-strung. If his books didn't balance to the penny, he made everyone's life a misery. There were times I could have killed him myself.

Collin Woodward, (the board member you met at my farewell gathering), was extremely relieved to hear that you could come straight away and double check Linley's reports.

I can't wait to see you. It's been donkey's years since we've shared a bottle.

E-mail me with your flight info. I was terribly sorry to hear about Shanna and Emma. When you're ready, we can talk.

Regards,

Douglas

After rereading the e-mail, Alec recalled the mixed feelings he had getting ready for his trip to the United States. After booking the flight, he gave Douglas the air carrier, flight number, and his expected time of arrival. His second and more difficult task was to ring his parents and say good-bye. They had been through so much lately.

It was well past midnight when Alec finished packing and got into bed. Even though he was eager to leave London, a part of him wanted to hold onto the memories that the city evoked. However, it was *those* memories that Alec needed to bury. They were just too numerous and too painful, often attacking him when he least expected.

Getting to Heathrow by seven was particularly hectic. While Alec packed last-minute items and printed off a second e-mail from Douglas, the cab driver impatiently announced his arrival by blasting his horn. Alec was unable to give the message more than a cursory glance until now.

Subj: Latest news on the Pegasus
Date: 22nd January, 11:13:42 PM EST

From: DAbbot953@Pegasus.com
To: AlecDunBarton@aol.com

Alec,

I'll make this one short.

I received your flight information and I'll meet you at Miami International Airport tomorrow afternoon. Look for me once you clear customs.

Don't be concerned if I'm a bit late. The homicide detectives will be inter-viewing crewmembers as soon as we dock in Port Everglades. I may also get tied up with the medical examiner or one of his staff.

I'll see you soon,

Douglas

With a heavy sigh and a final swallow of his drink, Alec put down his glass and correspondence. It wasn't a pretty picture. He wanted to make some notes—a plan of some kind. His body, though, had other ideas. Feeling overwhelmingly drowsy, Alec pulled down the plastic window shade, placed a pillow on top of it, and fell asleep.

Alec awoke to Amy's voice. "Mister, are you hungry? The flight attendant has chicken, beef, and a curry thing."

Alec always felt miserable after a nap. Sleeping in a cramped airline seat made him especially uncomfortable. His mouth was dry, and his neck and shoulders ached. He could do with some food. Carefully stretching his arms in front of him, he replied, "Beef will be fine."

The flight attendant placed his meal on the open tray. His lunch con-sisted of a leafy green salad, sliced beef in a red wine sauce, a medley of sautéed vegetables, dessert, and after-dinner cheese. The food wasn't too bad. But even after coffee and cheesecake, Alec felt hungry.

With nothing left to eat, Alec undid his seat belt and stood up. As he edged his way through the aisles, Alec watched his fellow passengers. Some of them were dozing, while others had their noses buried in books and magazines. Glimpsing toward the front of the plane, Alec could see their seatback video screens lit with different movies. Eager to get started on his project, he returned to his row, took his computer from the overhead compartment, and climbed over Amy who had fallen asleep.

Alec opened his laptop and began to list all the areas on the ship that collected additional revenue from its passengers. Since his days on the Delphinus, cruise lines had introduced many new moneymaking schemes.

In total, there were themed bars, exotic excursions, bingo, casino tables/slot machines, health/beauty treatments, fitness training, Internet fees, duty-free shops, and exclusive boutiques, not to mention specialty restaurants. To generate extra income per passenger, per day, it was the practice of cruise lines to set up specific monetary goals for each department to follow. Since it was the duty of the controller on Flagship Cruises to monitor the profit margin and keep HQ advised, Alec imagined that Mark Linley made several enemies among the crew.

It was one thing to make sure that each division gave an accurate account of its sales checks and properly maintained its inventory, but quite another to unearth a motive for murder. Thinking about the task that lay ahead, Alec became uneasy. He felt like a young lad about to attend his first day of school. Fortunately, his doubts passed quickly. He was skilled in following a money trail and even better at reading people. With some effort on his part, Alec thought he might be able to find a crucial piece of evidence.

CHAPTER 2

▼

"HERE COMES THE SUN"

Words & Music—George Harrison

Monday Afternoon—23rd of January

"Alec, Alec. I'm over here."

While Alec scanned the faces of the crowd waiting outside customs, Douglas stepped out from behind a chauffer and gave him a hearty hug.

"It's so good to see you my boy. How was your trip?"

Taking Alec's computer bag, Douglas continued, "Oh my God. Do you know *who* you look like?"

Alec's smile broadened. "Oh, not you too. You just saw me a few years ago. I've always looked like this. It's that Bond fellow who looks like me."

Douglas motioned Alec to follow him. "The garage is this way. It's lucky I had my car parked at the cruise terminal. I would have had to rent a car to collect you."

Before Alec could respond, they were outdoors in the blinding sunshine. Squinting at Douglas, Alec sang, "Here comes the sun, here comes the sun, And I say it's all right."

Amused, Douglas asked, "Are you still doing that?"

Alec grinned. "I know people think it's daft, but almost every word and event remind me of a song. At least, I'm a gifted tenor. It could be worse."

Realizing that his British retinas wouldn't be able to tolerate Floridian sunshine, Alec added, "Do you think we ought to stop for a pair of sunglasses? I didn't bring any."

"Don't worry," replied Douglas. "The ship's boutique is well stocked, and it will be open all day tomorrow."

After traversing through several rows of the car park, Douglas stopped in back of a white Hyundai Sonata with MD plates, opened the trunk, and put Alec's luggage inside. Alec placed his jacket on top of the bags and headed toward the left side of the car to get in.

Closing the trunk, Douglas looked up and laughed. "Are you driving?"

Alec glimpsed down and saw the steering wheel. Chuckling, he quipped, "I forgot the Yanks drive on the wrong side of the road."

On the thirty-five minute ride to Fort Lauderdale, they discussed their families. Douglas asked about Alec's parents. He and Alec's father, James DunBarton, had interned at the same hospital in London. Through the years, they'd often shared patients since James's specialty was gynecology and Douglas's internal medicine. Alec had originally met Dr. Douglas Abbot through his father.

Douglas retired five years ago when his wife died from lung cancer. She was a typical English wife who did everything for her husband, from laying out his clothing to arranging large dinner parties. Heartbroken after her death, Douglas relocated to Winter Park, Florida, to be close to his daughter's family who were living in Orlando. Though Douglas enjoyed retirement, he soon became bored with playing golf, swimming, and shopping.

It was a godsend when Douglas received an invitation from Collin, a former patient and board member of Flagship Cruise Line, to hire on as the physician for the Pegasus. Realizing that life at sea would be perfect for an elderly widower, Douglas signed a six-month contract. Between each term, the doctor had several months off to catch up with his family. Over the years, Douglas had come to be considered quite a catch among the gray-haired set of female passengers.

While Douglas drove and chatted about his daughter and grandchildren, Alec gave him an admiring glance. Somewhat jealous of the doctor's renewed lease on life, Alec hoped that his new venture would end his "long cold lonely winter."

Not ready to talk about Shanna and Emma, Alec spoke about his job at Royal Celtic Bank. Early in his career, Alec had been transferred from corporate headquarters in Edinburgh to its busy operations branch in London. Although he often traveled back and forth between England and Scotland, Alec didn't particularly mind. It afforded him an opportunity to see his relatives and former workmates. As Senior Internal Auditor, Alec enjoyed the challenge of solving numerical puzzles.

It was fortunate that Alec was already on an extended leave of absence from the bank when Douglas called him. Ultimately, he'd have to make a decision about returning to work. But for now, he had other things to consider.

Douglas turned off I-95 North to Griffin Road and remarked, "We'll be in Port Everglades in a few minutes. It's about five miles from here."

Alec was gazing out the window. The colors of Florida were mesmerizing. He couldn't get over the lush greens, sky blues, and brilliant pink and orange hues. It was as though he had stepped out of a black and white world into one of color.

Clearing his throat, Alec said, "I guess you'd better tell me what happened with the medical examiner and the homicide detectives."

Douglas replied grimly. "It was like watching one of those crime shows. The medical examiner's office sent a van to pick up Mark Linley's body. The attendant just wanted my report of the incident and his next of kin. He said that the forensic pathologist would get back to me when the autopsy was completed. I felt bloody useless."

Taking a breath, Douglas continued. "The crime scene technicians seemed to know their stuff. They inspected the gym from top to bottom searching for fibers, hairs, fingerprints, and blood. They found the murder weapon within seconds. They sprayed the dumbbells with a liquid called Luminol. One of the ten-pound weights lit up like a blue firefly on a dark night."

Alec was a fan of BBC crime dramas and had first seen Luminol in action on an episode of *Waking the Dead*. Wanting to know about the homicide detective, he asked, "Who's in charge?"

Douglas slowed down for traffic, and replied, "A man named Dan McGill. A few months ago, he investigated a case involving an Ecuadorian national who mysteriously died on a freighter. Even though the death was later ruled an accident, the detective became knowledgeable about jurisdictional matters. McGill assures us that the Pegasus will be leaving on time or close to it. When we get back to the ship, I expect he'll be concluding his interviews with the staff."

As Douglas turned into the entrance of the port, he announced, "We're here now."

He stopped at a gate to show his ship's identification card to a sheriff at the checkpoint and headed for the long-term parking garage. After taking a ticket from the machine at the entrance of the car lot, Douglas found a convenient spot on the third level. The two men quickly emptied the trunk and walked over to the section of the terminal for crewmembers.

Alec nearly got writer's cramp filling in forms. By fax, Douglas was able to obtain documentation from headquarters that designated Alec as a temporary officer. Once Douglas presented those papers along with Alec's passport to the officials, they were allowed to board.

It was ten past 3:00 P.M. when they stepped onto the ship. Douglas showed Alec to his cabin so that he could wash up before meeting the others. Before entering the room with the plastic key card, Alec asked tentatively, "This wasn't Linley's cabin, was it?"

Douglas smiled at his discomfort. "No, his stateroom is on the starboard side. It was being dusted for fingerprints when I left for the airport. They plan to keep his cabin sealed for a while."

Hastily, the doctor handed Alec his carryon bag. "I promised to let Captain Jarvis know when we arrived. I'll be back to collect you in say thirty minutes?"

Equally anxious to get to the bathroom, Alec replied, "Fine with me," and quickly disappeared behind the door.

Half an hour later, Alec was cleanly shaven and properly attired. He felt like a new man. When Alec started to unpack his suitcase, he found three sets of uniforms hanging in his closet. Like the chair sizes presented in the fairy tale, *The Three Bears*, one uniform fit perfectly.

The officer's finery consisted of a white short-sleeve shirt, white trousers, and a pair of deck shoes. Alec was especially fascinated with the two black and gold stripes that were embroidered on his epaulet. He had to stop admiring himself long enough to respond to the knock at his door.

"Come on in," he called, still glancing at his reflection in the mirror.

Douglas gave Alec the once over and grinned. "Don't we look handsome?"

Alec noticed that Douglas had changed as well. Their uniforms were exactly alike except Douglas, as ship's physician, had three stripes on his sleeve.

Following the doctor out of his stateroom, Alec asked, "So what's on the agenda this evening?"

"Well," answered Douglas, "The captain wants us to have a word with the homicide detective. Moments ago, McGill finished interviewing Gwen Llewelyn, the fitness instructor, who discovered Mark Linley's body in the gym. The detectives have been using the Dolphin Lounge as their base of operations. The room is just down the hall.

"After that, there's a senior staff meeting at the movie theatre on the Promenade Deck. By that time, the passengers will be returning from their lifeboat drill and getting ready for the sail-away party. Jarvis wants to stop ship scuttlebutt before it gets out of hand."

In the corridor, Douglas gave Alec a map of the ship. "Here, I think you'll need this until you become acclimated."

Smiling, Alec folded it in half and tucked it away.

The Dolphin Room appeared empty when they looked in, and Douglas thought it prudent to wait outside. Observing two men walking toward them, Alec whispered, "Is one of them McGill?"

Douglas quickly told him who was who.

As the detectives drew closer, Alec had a chance to size up McGill. He wasn't what he imagined. McGill was thin, short, and rather wiry. There was nothing really striking about his appearance, but Alec got the impression he was *all* business.

Upon entering the lounge, Alec's attention was drawn to the odd assortment of furniture in the room. There was a large-screen TV, fax machine, refrigerator, and gold-plated coffee urn, which stood beside a nearly empty tray of cookies. A floor-to-ceiling bookcase stood against one wall, displaying some hardcover books and a wide selection of dog-eared paperbacks. There was even an edition of *Encyclopedia Britannica*.

The chairs and sofa appeared comfortable and lived in. Alec could see himself happily ensconced in one of the soft-looking leather couches.

Detective McGill invited them to take a seat at a rectangular wooden table that occupied the center of the room. The table had signs of recent use. It was covered with tall plastic glasses, china coffee cups, cookie crumbs, and soiled paper napkins.

Once they were settled, McGill formally introduced himself and took their names. He then instructed his partner to start the tape recorder and announced, "This interview is strictly a means to gather preliminary information about the victim."

Gazing directly at Alec, he continued. "As long as the doctor doesn't have any objections, I'd like you to remain here while I speak to Dr. Abbot. My superiors tell me that you'll be auditing the controller's books for irregularities."

Alec nodded his head in assent. Directing his inquiry to Douglas, McGill asked, "Would you mind if Mr. DunBarton sits in?"

Douglas replied curtly, "Of course not," and Alec wondered why he sounded so miffed.

McGill began to fire a series of questions at the doctor. Did he known Mark Linley before joining this ship? How many years did they serve together? Did he like him? Had they ever argued? Alec was particularly interested in Douglas's responses to the last two questions, since he mentioned that the controller often drove him crazy.

Douglas answered all the detective's inquires in his finest Queen's English. When asked about their relationship, the doctor replied that he found Linley "a nervous chap" and "rather annoying." Douglas admitted that he had locked horns with him over their last inventory of medicine and medical supplies.

McGill demanded, "What happened?"

Douglas thought a moment and replied, "About three weeks ago, Linley shouted at one of my nurses when he discovered we were short a box of tongue depressors. I had given the box to a child to play with while I set his mother's broken arm and forgot to tell Nora to remove it from the inventory list. Mark Linley's crude remarks upset her, and I felt responsible. Frankly, I lost my temper and told him to bugger off."

Alec choked down a laugh as McGill asked his final question, "When was the last time you saw the victim alive?"

"It was Saturday night, the evening before his death. A group of us sat with Linley and his assistant Scott Harris at a table in the Lido Restaurant. I was with Beth, my other nurse, and Gwen, the fitness director."

"Go on," prompted McGill.

"Well, Linley and Harris appeared to be in a heated argument when we joined them. After dinner, Rick Tanner, the cruise director, came along with his fiancée Janet Kane. We had dessert and coffee. Linley looked preoccupied, and Gwen was unusually quiet. When the controller left the table, I heard him mutter something about a "bottle.""

McGill simply said, "Satisfactory" and stood up.

The detective brusquely thanked Douglas, and stated that he and his team would be leaving the ship soon. He then turned his attention to Alec. "Mr. DunBarton, can you remain with me a moment?"

Douglas took his cue to leave and told Alec that he'd wait for him by the forward elevators. Seconds later, McGill's partner departed to find out whether the crime scene unit was packed up.

Once the door closed, the detective turned off the tape recorder and removed a loose sheet of paper from behind the officer's notebook.

McGill handed Alec a list of names. "I'm afraid this case may not be solved as quickly as I had anticipated. The victim made a lot of enemies. I'll be doing background checks on everyone that I interviewed today, along with some of the passengers. If we're lucky, the lab boys may turn up traces of DNA on the dumbbell. In the meantime, I want you to scrutinize the financial records of the people on this list and get back to me."

Alec glimpsed at the names and acknowledged he would. McGill continued, "Please e-mail me any information that appears out of the ordinary. I need you to be my eyes and ears onboard the Pegasus since my legal jurisdiction is limited. I'll send you updates on my investigation as well."

The two men exchanged e-mail addresses and shook hands. Alec saw McGill smile for the first time as they parted outside the lounge.

Alec began to walk to his right, hoping he was headed for the service elevators. Dressed in official regalia, he thought it would look rather strange staring at a diagram of the ship. Further up the corridor, Alec spotted Douglas and asked, "How are we doing on time?"

"They just announced the passenger life boat drill." Pressing the elevator button, he added, "Let's get going. We don't want to keep the captain waiting."

CHAPTER 3

▼

"ONE WAY OR ANOTHER"

Words & Music—Deborah Harry and Nigel Harrison

Tuesday Morning—24th of January

At 6:00 A.M, the clock alarm ushered in Alec's first day at sea. The gentle rocking of the ship had acted like a bottle of Scotch without its disagreeable side effects, and Alec slept like a baby.

Not one to shower right away, Alec slipped on his robe and tottered off to the Dolphin Room for a large cup of coffee. He was glad that no one was in the corridor to see his state of undress. The coffee smelled delicious, but he was disappointed to learn that there were only small china cups stacked beside the urn. Alec needed an oversized mug to fully wake up. After stuffing a few cookies in the pocket of his tartan bathrobe, Alec prepared two coffees with creamer.

He managed to get back to the room without spilling too many drops. Alec placed the cups on his end table and made himself comfortable. He removed his robe, settled back into bed, and turned on the television using the remote. There wasn't any cable on the ship since the Pegasus was a *floating* hotel. Surfing through the channels, Alec found a live satellite news program along with several piped in movie and music stations. For passengers who didn't know what to do with themselves, there were also shows devoted to shipboard events. In the mood for music, Alec selected a pop rock station. Relaxing against his propped up pillows, he began his first cup.

Sipping appreciatively, Alec looked around his cabin. He was grateful that he didn't have to share his quarters. The noncommissioned crew on the lower decks often slept two or more to a room. The cabin was certainly colorful and shipshape. The twin beds were covered in a bright turquoise, coral, and yellow batik fabric that coordinated with the curtains and décor.

Alec spent his first night in the bed to the right of the door, deciding to let the other one serve as a couch. Between the bed and couch, he had a handy nightstand that held his coffees, telephone, and television remote. Natural light came in from a porthole just above the end table. The television set hung discreetly from the ceiling and it was positioned perfectly for Alec to watch from bed. With ample closet space, a table and chairs, and a full bathroom, Alec was certain he'd be content in Cabin 946.

As Alec took the cookies from his robe pocket, he removed the lint and popped them in his mouth. To him, they were biscuits. In any case, they were gone in moments. Deciding to transfer McGill's list of possible suspects to his computer, Alec reached for his laptop.

While Alec was typing in the last name, someone knocked at the door. Not having locked it after his coffee raid, Alec shouted, "Come in." Belatedly, he hoped it wasn't the murderer or the captain. He wasn't dressed properly for either.

Fortunately, it was a cabin steward carrying in several more white uniforms. As he closed the door quietly behind him, he said, "I would like to introduce myself to you. My name is Widarta, but you can call me Widi. Everyone does. I will be cleaning your cabin." Unobtrusively, he placed the garments in the full-length closet.

Alec liked the young man immediately. Remembering he was clad in only boxer shorts, Alec remained in bed. "I'm glad to meet you Widi. My name is Alec."

Widarta smiled. "Is there anything that I can get you?"

With nothing coming to mind, Alec shook his head. "No. But thanks for bringing me new clothes. I wasn't sure my uniform was still clean."

Widarta scanned the room and gathered up Alec's shirt and trousers, which were draped over a chair. As he opened the door to leave, he said, "I'll have them washed and ironed for you."

Alec had one more name to remember, but he felt sure he wouldn't forget the cabin steward's. Glancing at the list of names he just entered in his database, Alec began to review his evening.

He and Douglas arrived at the captain's meeting as it started. There were approximately forty officers and staff members in attendance. Not wanting to draw attention to themselves, Alec and Douglas sat toward the rear of the cinema.

The captain, Nigel Jarvis, spoke with a determined air. "At this time, I haven't any *new* information on the sad death of the controller. I want you all to do your best to return a sense of normalcy to this vessel. The welfare and safety of our passengers are to remain our primary concern. I know you have questions. For the time being, take your accounting queries to Scott Harris, the Assistant Controller, and continue to bring issues of security to Officer Ronald Bauer."

Looking to his left, the captain motioned the security officer to come into view and speak. Jarvis, who was tall and athletic-looking, towered over the chief of security. In contrast to the well-tanned captain, the officer was not only short in stature, but also extremely pale-skinned.

With a German accent, Bauer stated, "The fitness, health, and beauty staff can now return to the spa. The detectives and crime scene unit have left the ship."

Although no one clapped, Alec felt emotional applause. The tension in the room dropped dramatically. Bauer continued, "I'd now like to call up Alec DunBarton, if he's here." Heads turned as Alec rose and walked to the front of the theatre.

Even now, quietly sitting in bed, Alec relived the surprise of hearing his name mentioned and his subsequent introduction. Both Captain Jarvis and Bauer greeted him warmly, and the captain announced to the gathering that Alec's position on the Pegasus would be that of Liaison Officer. The captain added that Alec would be responsible for ongoing communication between the crew of the Pegasus and the Sheriff's Department.

Anyone with information, questions, or concerns about Mark Linley's death was to contact Alec DunBarton at the controller's office.

Starting on his second cup of coffee, Alec clearly saw the politics of the situation. No one wanted to be left holding the bag or the body in this case. If the murderer turned out to be one of the passengers, there'd be a collective sigh of relief. However, if one of the crew had done the deed, it would reflect poorly on the cruise line and the reputations of its officers. As an outsider, Alec had the least to lose. He was expendable.

After the captain's meeting ended, several people came up to Alec. One young woman in a salon coat appeared especially eager to talk to him and waited for the others to leave. When a voice on the intercom announced that the sail-away party was about to begin, she disappeared. Alec hoped he'd be able to speak to her in the next few days.

By the time Alec finished greeting many of his new coworkers, he was exhausted. Since it was almost 10:30 P.M. in England, Douglas suggested a quick supper in the Lido Restaurant. Over dinner, they evaluated the captain's meeting, and watched the growing distance between the ship and its port. When Alec returned to his cabin, he fell asleep as soon as his head touched the pillow.

With his lukewarm coffee finished, Alec decided to shower, have breakfast, and review Mark's weekly reports. As he headed toward the bathroom, Alec heard Blondie's voice coming from the television singing, "One way or another, I'm gonna find ya,' I'm gonna get ya', get ya', get ya, get ya.'" Her voice made him stop in his tracks.

Alec wasn't sure whether there was a God, especially lately. But as he listened to the lyrics, he felt compelled to do more than check financial records. McGill wanted him to be his "eyes and ears" on the ship. The captain and the security chief seemed anxious to relinquish their responsibility. A man had been viciously murdered.

Then and there, Alec swore to do everything in his power to reveal the killer's identity. To him, it represented a way to regain control of *his* life and to stop running away from the past.

Even at 7:00 in the morning, the Lido Deck was congested with hungry passengers. Alec supposed it was because the formal dining room hadn't yet opened. While searching for a free table, Alec was invited to sit with a young blonde woman who appeared to be one of the fitness instructors. He wished her nameplate were larger and placed higher on her warm-up jacket. Alec didn't want her to think he was staring at her chest. As she pulled out his chair, she said, "You're the Liaison Officer aren't you? I saw you last night. I'm Gwen."

Alec immediately recognized the name. She was present at Mark Linley's "last supper" and later discovered his body in the gym.

Eager to speak to her, Alec deposited his plate of scrambled eggs and hash browns on the table, and extended his hand. "Yes. I'm Alec DunBarton. I was hoping to meet you."

She grasped his hand and held it quite a while before releasing it. Provocatively, she murmured, "Mmm, it's a real *pleasure* to make your acquaintance."

Alec took the offered seat and wondered whether Gwen was usually this playful with everyone. While he tried to form an opinion, he said, "I have a couple of questions. Do you have time to answer them now?"

Deciding that she probably used flirtation as a defense mechanism, Alec didn't wait for a reply. Instead, he gazed directly into her clear blue eyes and asked, "Did you kill Mark Linley?"

Her nostrils flared and her bottom lip quivered as she blurted out, "I'm not sorry he was murdered. He could be very mean. I didn't do it, but lots of people on this ship wished he were dead."

"Like who?"

"Scott, for starters."

"Who else?"

"Paige hated Mark's guts."

"Can you think of any others?"

"Oh, everyone. He always acted like he was so perfect. Well, he wasn't."

Not wanting her to stop talking, Alec asked, "Can you tell me what happened on Saturday night when you dined with Linley?"

Recovering herself, Gwen looked at him blankly and said, "I can't remember much." After some prodding, she echoed the doctor's opinion that Mark and Scott were arguing, an activity that occurred pretty regularly. She didn't hear Mark Linley mention the word *bottle*, but admitted she really wasn't paying attention. Earlier that day, she fought with her boyfriend, Boyd Griffin, one of the ship's musicians.

Suspecting that the argument with her friend caused her, in Douglas's words, to be "unusually quiet," Alec asked, "Was anything else bothering you?"

Unprepared for her blunt response, Alec nearly dropped a forkful of egg. With a torrent of unladylike words, Gwen proceeded to call Rick's fiancée almost every name in the book, including some that that were unprintable. She ended her tirade with, "Rick could do a lot better."

At this point, Alec became confused. Why was she upset about this Rick and his girlfriend, if she had a boyfriend?

Deciding to table that line of inquiry until he had some background information, Alec asked her about finding the body. Even though she seemed reluctant to go on, she shrugged her shoulders as if to say, "Okay you win."

Briefly, she explained, "The spa opens for fitness instruction at 6:00. On Sunday, it was my turn to go in early. When I walked into the reception area, I noticed the door to the gym was kind of open. At the time, I didn't think anything of it. Like always, I went in, turned up the lights, and checked the towels."

Pulling on her bottom lip, she quickly added, "Then I noticed the lid of the Alpha Capsule was shut, and there was blood all over the place. Mark's face was bashed in, and I ran back to receptionist's desk to call security."

While Alec tried to absorb everything he just heard, Gwen abruptly rose from her chair. Apologetically, she declared, "I have to go now. My aerobics class is at eight."

Before leaving, she managed to give Alec a coquettish smile and cooed, "Come up and see me sometime." Alec doubted she had ever heard Mae West's famous line, so he simply agreed he would.

Glancing at his cold, half-eaten breakfast, Alec decided to visit the doctor right away. Last evening, Douglas mentioned that he'd be in the infirmary all morning, seeing passengers who had forgotten to bring along their motion sickness medicine. Armed with a dozen questions, Alec made his way down to the Marine Deck.

Not sure whether to knock, Alec peered into the infirmary. A nurse was bent over a kitchen worker, applying ointment to his finger. Alec didn't want to disturb them, so he waited several minutes for her to look up. Receiving no greeting, he finally asked for Dr. Abbot. With a scowl and a brisk nod of her head, she indicated he was in his office. As he walked across the room, Alec wondered whether she was the nurse who had attended Mark's supper party.

Douglas stood at the inner office door with a big grin on his face. Closing the door behind them, he said, "I see you met my drill sergeant."

"She's rather brusque. Which one of the two nurses is she?"

Douglas replied, "Neither. That's Maggie Hart. Although her bedside manner needs improvement, she's a first-rate physician's assistant. It was Nora Sheffield who argued with Linley, and Beth Romano who was my dinner companion on Saturday evening."

Amused, Alec teased, "You have quite a harem."

"Other than spying on my staff, what can I do for you?"

Alec settled into a soft leather chair in the corner of his office. The room looked like a library, with stacks of medical books and journals neatly arranged in tall bookcases. Douglas took a seat behind his large, polished-oak desk that displayed photos of his wife and daughter. Two additional chairs were positioned directly in front of the desk to serve as a consultation area. The doctor's faded diplomas hung on the wall, along with prints of old sailing vessels.

For a moment, Alec wished he had his pipe. But he doubted that Maggie would permit such a breach of protocol in her sick bay.

Instead, he asked, "Can you give me some paper?"

"Is that all you wanted?"

"No my friend, I need information. Lots of it." Taking a legal pad from the doctor's outstretched hand and a pen from his desk, Alec started to ask questions. "First of all, who is Paige, and why did she hate Mark Linley?"

Douglas leaned back, appearing ready for a lengthy discussion. "The only Paige onboard is Paige Anderson, the cruise consultant. She assists passengers in booking their next cruise. I hadn't heard there was any bad blood between her and Mark. It's possible they once served together. Paige has been with the company for well over fifteen years, and Linley made a habit of transferring from one ship to another."

Alec was excited by the news. Paige Anderson wasn't on McGill's list and she might have had a relationship with Mark. Wanting to know more, Alec demanded, "Tell me, what's she like?"

"Well, let's see," Douglas replied, apparently collecting his thoughts.

"Paige is attractive. She's quite tall with short red hair that always looks sort of wind swept. She's divorced and in her forties. To tell you the truth, I find her a bit of an enigma. She's friendly, but manages to keep her distance from everyone. You can meet her tonight at the Captain's Welcome Reception. Paige is one of the few female officers on the Pegasus."

Alec's eyes twinkled as he said, "I wonder whether she could pass up the charms of a handsome Scottish gentleman."

Douglas grinned at Alec's hubris. "If you want to catch her eye tonight, you'd better resemble your pal Pierce. You've been looking rather average in your uniform."

Still curious, Alec asked Douglas about Rick Tanner and Janet Kane. Luckily, Maggie was capable of handling all the patients for the next hour. In that time, Alec got an earful and took plenty of notes. He learned that Rick had been in a few off Broadway shows before turning his talents to cruise directing. It was rumored that he came from a wealthy family and earned *more* than the captain. Douglas added that Rick had a way with the opposite sex and might have been seeing Gwen on the sly.

When Douglas described Rick's fiancée, Janet Kane, Alec detected a note of adoration in his voice. To the doctor, she was a petite beauty with delicate features, "a radiant creature." Alec could well understand Gwen's strong language if she had been thrown over by Rick.

Douglas went on to explain that Janet had become a frequent passenger on the Pegasus since becoming engaged to Rick during the Thanksgiving Cruise. The happy couple planned to tie the knot in Barbados in April when the Southern Dreams' Tour ended. Since Janet owned a travel agency, she was able to take time off work to visit Rick and make wedding preparations. Even though she wasn't on this cruise, Douglas appeared quite gleeful when he remarked that Janet would be joining them next Wednesday when the ship set sail again.

Getting off the topic of his ladylove, Alec asked about Gwen. Douglas readily agreed that Miss Llewelyn was a flirt, but remarked that Boyd was a good influence on her. Both she and Boyd were blonde, tall, and slender, and seemed quite suited to each other. Douglas was sure that they'd make up sooner or later.

His questions answered, and his body stiff from sitting, Alec thanked the doctor. As he rose from the chair, he inquired, "Will the captain be showing you off at tonight's festivities?"

"Of course," responded Douglas suavely. "He wants his passengers to meet his amiable and accomplished physician. Have you been invited for the lineup?"

Alec laughed. "By God, I hope not. I'd look bloody ridiculous being presented to the gathering as a Straw Man hunting for a murderous crew-member."

"That's true," Douglas chortled, "As our new Liaison Officer, that wouldn't go over too well."

They quickly made arrangements to meet right after the reception so that Alec could be formally introduced to Paige Anderson. Alec tore off his notes from the legal pad and made his way out of the infirmary. He was grateful that the names on the paper were beginning to take on a persona, and that Maggie was occupied with a patient.

Although it was only ten o'clock, Alec was feeling peckish after his curtailed breakfast. Since lunch on the Lido Deck wouldn't be served for another thirty minutes, Alec decided to visit the shopping arcade to purchase a mug and sunglasses.

Recalling that cash wasn't used on cruise ships, Alec stopped off at the Front Desk to activate his onboard account with a credit card. Within moments, Alec's plastic room key also became his shipboard currency.

The controller's office was to the right of the reception area. Since he was in the neighborhood, Alec decided to try the handle and see whether anyone was inside.

A distinguished looking officer was seated at a desk behind a computer screen. The man glanced up at Alec and appeared to recognize him. As he got to his feet, he said, "I'm Scott Harris. I'm pleased to meet you."

While Alec shook his hand, he studied his features. Harris had sad brown eyes and a neatly clipped gray moustache. Alec placed his accent to be Jamaican.

Apparently, Scott was told to expect the Liaison Officer and to give him access to the files. He showed Alec the inner office where Mark Linley had worked. Expecting to see recent signs of use and fingerprint dust, Alec was amazed to see neither. Mark's desk was completely void of trays, writing implements, and other bookkeeping essentials, not to mention a computer.

Scott explained that the police took everything and the cleaning crew later removed all traces of forensic activity.

Alec silently wondered what in the world he'd review and asked whether there was any backup material. Scott enthusiastically assured him that there were hard copies of every report and inventory list, as well as sales checks dating back three years. Mark had chronically worried that one of them would pick up a computer virus. Scott showed him a massive cabinet of files that were cross-referenced by date and department.

Although the controller's desk was barren, Alec felt amused and reassured that there was enough documentation to keep him busy for months.

After conversing awhile, Alec told Scott that he'd be returning to the office after lunch to begin his audit. Scott visibly stiffened in response to his words, and Alec asked himself why. Was he hiding something or just concerned that the Liaison Officer would uncover a slight computational error in one of his reports? Scott Harris appeared to be a decent chap, but Alec made a mental note to thoroughly go over his work.

Before leaving, Scott handed him a key and stated that he would be in the wine "cellar" all afternoon taking an inventory of its contents. He promised to leave his computer on in case Alec needed to download any recent files.

With his stomach grumbling from hunger, Alec decided to visit the shops later. Frustrated that all the elevators were engaged on other floors, Alec loped up four flights of stairs to the restaurant.

Well fed and satisfied with life in general, Alec completed several errands. Undeterred this time, Alec made it to the shopping arcade. After looking around for a few minutes, he bought himself a pair of sunglasses, a bottle of suntan lotion, a round tin of Scottish butter cookies, and an inordinately large coffee mug embossed with the Pegasus logo. His next stop was his cabin to unload his goodies and pick up his laptop.

Even though his bed looked inviting for an afternoon nap, Alec splashed cold water on his face instead. Ready to examine the sales checks and the monetary targets of the fitness club, Alec headed off to his squeaky clean office.

CHAPTER 4

▼

"THINGS ARE LOOKING UP"

Words & Music—George and Ira Gershwin

Tuesday Afternoon—24th of January

By three thirty, Alec was tired of numbers. So far, his investigation had revealed several interesting facts. In order to confirm his theory, Alec needed to see Officer Bauer or visit the ship's photo lab. Not wanting to step on any toes, he decided to speak to the chief of security first.

Alec closed his computer and locked it in the drawer. Mark's desk would be left in pristine condition. He added the key to the ring that Scott gave him earlier. Alec was thankful that the controller's outer door required an old fashioned metal key. There was something comforting about the sound it made when it turned in the lock. The noise also served to make Alec aware of another inconsistency in the case.

Not knowing the extension for the security officer, Alec walked to the Front Desk to have him paged. He hoped Bauer would be available. Once Alec conceived a plan, he liked to follow it through to its conclusion. He suspected that most accountants wanted people and numbers to add up.

Gazing in the direction of the grand staircase, Alec was pleased to see Bauer heading toward him. Although, he spent some time with him after the captain's meeting, Alec still found his ghost-like appearance unsettling.

Bauer explained he had fifteen minutes to spare and asked Alec to join him for tea in the Churchill Room. Ready for a snack, Alec gladly accepted.

The two found a freshly set table overlooking the ocean. In his excitement of pursuing a murderer, Alec had forgotten to admire the beauty and majesty of the sea. He made a note to himself to treasure these moments. Life could change dramatically.

The waiter immediately brought a tray of little sandwiches, scones, and cream cakes. After he chose several of each, Alec looked up slightly abashed. His companion had selected just two sandwiches. Another waiter was right behind the first with a pot of tea, milk, sugar, and lemon. Bauer took his tea plain. Alec always liked his strong with milk. He was not disappointed. Once the teatime niceties were completed, Bauer took a sip of his hot beverage and asked, "How are you making out?"

Alec stuffed a sandwich in his mouth before replying. "Oh, I'm doing fine. Would you mind if I asked you a few questions?"

"Go ahead."

"First off, do you know whether the controller had a key to the fitness area?"

Bauer stared at his tea with a perplexed expression. "He was never issued one, and no one was permitted in the spa after hours. I wondered how he had gained access."

"Did you find a key on him?"

Bauer shook his head. "It's possible he had one in his trousers, but the sheriff's office told us to leave his body alone."

"Were any keys reported lost or stolen?"

"They're all accounted for. I gave Gwen a duplicate about two months ago. She told me she lost hers while she was conducting a dancercise class on the beach in Coral Cay. Should I be concerned?"

Removing whipped cream from his top lip, Alec replied, "No, not at all. When we return to port, I'll ask McGill whether he found a key on his body, and we can take it from there."

Changing the subject, Alec remarked, "I heard you took snapshots of the crime scene for the police. Did you happen to make any copies?"

"I did photograph the area, and it was ghastly. As chief of security, I've had to investigate petty thefts, stop fights among the crew, and sometimes deal with the death of an elderly passenger. But, I've never been associated with a cold-blooded murder. It's really unthinkable.

"As to your question," Bauer continued, "I believe all the photos were given to the homicide detective. Alfie, one of the photo lab boys, developed them for me. He still may have the negatives. I'm headed in that direction. You can ask him yourself."

Alec was sure that the police had taken those too. But knowing human nature, Alec thought it possible that Alfie made copies to sell to the tabloids. Keeping that to himself, Alec downed the last drop of tea and followed Bauer out.

The printing lab was deep in the bowels of the ship. Alec was glad to have an escort there and equally pleased that Bauer carried on to the engine room.

As Alec entered the facility, he was astonished by its size. On one side of the chamber there were several large developing and enlarging machines. The other side of the room contained a busy publication center, which printed the ship's daily newspaper, programs, menus, trivia forms, spa specials, and tour fliers.

Alec approached a young man who was sorting photographs on a long counter. Seeing the uniform, the boy straightened up and asked, "Can I help you?"

"I was hoping to find Alfie. Is he here?"

"I'm Alfie," he replied tentatively.

With the young man's identity confirmed, Alec went into his spiel. Exaggerating his importance slightly, Alec explained he was working directly with the Sheriff's Office and was there to pick up shots of the crime scene.

Noting surprise and a bit of fear in his eyes, Alec stated, "Now laddy, I know you have extras. Give them to me, and we won't say another word about it." Alfie looked as though he were about to explain, but shrugged his shoulders instead.

After disappearing behind a cabinet, he returned with a large manila envelope. As he handed it to Alec, he said, "Look sir, I'm sorry. I meant no harm."

Alec smiled reassuringly. "Get back to work, son. It's forgotten."

With the pictures safely tucked under his arm, Alec cautiously retraced his steps back to his cabin. He didn't have time to get lost. It was getting late, and he needed to shower, shave, and dress for the early seating of the Captain's Welcome Reception.

Half an hour later, a very dapper Liaison Officer set off for the Starlight Lounge—the dazzling two-level 500-passenger auditorium. Alec's formal attire consisted of a long-sleeve white shirt with mandarin collar, a thin black bowtie, black trousers, and a short white cutaway jacket.

Alone in the elevator, Alec glimpsed at his smiling expression in the mirrored doors and sang aloud, "Things are looking up. I've been looking the landscape over, And it's covered with four leaf clover. Oh things are looking up." Just as he uttered "looking up," the elevator opened and a rather elderly couple got on. Alec continued to hum while the pair focused their attention straight ahead. There was no doubt that Alec was feeling pleased with himself and "his case."

The Starlight Lounge was practically filled to capacity. Waiters and waitresses were hovering around tables delivering fluted glasses of champagne, red wine, and fruit punch. The hors d'oeuvres were less numerous, but Alec managed to commandeer a few of them from a passing tray. He found an empty seat facing far right of the stage.

The captain and several officers were already on the podium. None of the faces seemed familiar. While Alec was asking for some punch, he nearly missed the doctor's grand entrance upon the stage. Alec glanced up when he heard "Douglas Abbot, ship's physician."

Behind Douglas was a striking redhead in a long white sequined gown. The captain introduced her as "Paige Anderson, future-cruise consultant." After seeing her in person, Alec became more eager than ever to interview her that evening. He was a man with a mission.

Once everyone was presented, Captain Jarvis asked Rick Tanner, the cruise director, to join them on stage. A dark slender man jumped onto the platform and took the microphone from Jarvis. With enthusiasm overflowing, Tanner urged the audience to attend the grand musical extravaganza, which was scheduled after dinner. He also told "late-night revelers," they could dance the night away at the Constellation Lounge.

This was Alec's first view of Tanner. Even though Alec was at least thirty feet from the cruise director, the small hairs on the back of his neck stood on end. To Alec, Rick looked artificial and slick. He would never buy a used car from him, but he knew he'd enjoy interrogating him.

With the festivities at an end, the captain and his officers began to exit the stage. At the end of his row, Alec waited for the doctor and Paige to come down the aisle. On seeing Alec, Douglas turned to Paige and said, "Oh. Let me introduce you to my good friend, Alec DunBarton. He's currently serving as our Liaison Officer."

Alec closed the distance between them and warmly extended his hand. "I'm glad to meet you. I was wondering whether we could have a quiet chat later on."

Paige seemed surprised by his words. Alec surmised that she hadn't heard about his role in the murder inquiry. Many of the officers and staff were required to be present at the passenger lifeboat drill the previous afternoon and missed the captain's meeting.

Apparently flattered by his invitation, Paige responded, "That would be lovely."

After Alec made arrangements to meet Paige at the Zodiac Bar at nine, he and Douglas went to dinner. The carved meat section of the buffet had prime rib. With a full plate of medium rare roast beef, buttered new potatoes, and Brussels spouts almandine, Alec was in seventh heaven. Douglas chose stuffed flounder in a cream sauce. Although fish was the freshest on the first few days of the cruise, Alec found it impossible to pass up a good cut of meat.

Noting the limited seating in the restaurant, they grabbed an outside table that overlooked the pool. Douglas let Alec eat for several minutes before asking him about his day. It was hard to get an answer from Alec with his mouth full. When he finally slowed down, the doctor said, "So, what did you find out?"

Alec took a swallow of lemonade and replied, "Well, for starters, I examined the sales receipts of the spa gym. Linley used the Alpha Capsule regularly. Every week, he purchased a 90-minute package for eighty dollars. Then in mid November, he suddenly stopped buying time on the machine."

Alec waited a moment to see whether the doctor understood what he was saying. Douglas had a rather blank expression on his face and merely said, "Go on."

"Two other things happened during that period. After checking the stats for the fitness center, I noticed that Mark Linley lowered Gwen's monetary goals. That part of the spa makes its money from Pilates, yoga, and kickboxing classes, as well as personal fitness instruction, body composition analysis, and diet consultations. It seems that your controller made a dirty deal with Gwen."

"How do you know it was with her and not the male fitness director?"

"Elementary my dear doctor," echoed Alec in the words of Sherlock Holmes. "About two months ago, Gwen told Bauer she lost her key to the fitness center. I think she gave the duplicate to Linley so he could come and go as he pleased. I also looked at the crime scene photos. There was no way Gwen could have identified the controller in that bloody state. She assumed it was him, knowing he made use of the Alpha Capsule when the gym was closed."

Now playing the part of Dr. Watson, Douglas exclaimed, "Well done!" Concern for Gwen then took over. "Do you think she killed him?"

"A woman could have done it. A ten-pound weight causes a lot of damage, and Gwen is certainly fit enough to wield it effectively."

Sensing it was time to change the topic, Alec announced that he was ready for dessert and coffee. The two men talked of more pleasant things until 7:30 when Douglas took his leave to check on a patient who had experienced chest pains earlier.

With an hour and a half to kill before meeting Paige, Alec returned to his office to examine her financial records.

As the Liaison Officer, Alec wasn't certain how many hours he was expected to put in. Typically a controller worked from 8:00 A.M. to 2:00 P.M. and 5:00 P.M. to 9:00 P.M. seven days a week. Alec knew his mind would be occupied with details of the case well past "normal" working hours.

From a floppy disk, Alec was able to retrieve the monthly fees that had been charged to each crewmember's onboard account. After looking over Paige's purchases, Alec was able to form a somewhat accurate picture of the cruise consultant. She often visited the spa and spent money on back massages and hair care. Paige was also quite fond of gin and tonic, and her favorite hot spot was the Lido Lounge.

Still curious about her relationship with the controller, Alec began to check her statistics. He was a little disappointed to learn that they were exemplary. Mark had set fair goals, and Paige consistently surpassed his targets. Alec's only recourse was to go over her employment history with the human resource department in London. Since it would take days to get a response by e-mail, Alec decided he would have to use a little deception.

Alec entered the Zodiac Bar at a quarter to nine and was immediately impressed by its ambience and décor. The lighting was muted and the tables were situated in cozy little alcoves along the window. On the walls, there were plaques of the twelve astrological symbols. A trio of jazz musicians was just setting up to play in the corner of the room. Not sure whether the music would be too loud, Alec selected a table a suitable distance away. He hated to raise his voice while he was trying to be charming.

As the group began to play "The Girl from Ipanema," Alec noticed Paige at the entrance of the lounge. She was still attired in her form-fitting evening gown, and Alec thought her quite stunning. In order to be seen, he stood up and watched her weave her way through the tables.

A waiter appeared at the same instant that Paige arrived and took their orders. Alec wasn't surprised to hear her order gin and tonic with a twist of lime. On learning that the ship carried his much-loved Glenlivet, Alec was able to fully relax. He couldn't imagine anything worse than being stranded in the middle of the Caribbean without a decent whisky.

When the waiter left, Alec said, "So, tell me about yourself."

Appearing uncertain as to where to begin, she smiled weakly. "What would you like to know?"

"Since we're in the Zodiac Bar, tell me your sign. Or better yet, let me guess it."

Warming to the game, Paige asked, "Do you need any clues?"

Alec had delved into astrology when he was a young lad. He knew how to construct a birth chart, but wasn't especially good at reading the planets or understanding their meaning. With some rudimentary knowledge and a little luck, he thought he might be able to figure out Paige's sun sign and discover more about her.

Just as Alec was about to pose his questions, the waiter delivered their drinks with a small complementary plate of appetizers. For once, Alec was more interested in talking than eating. He raised his glass and made a toast. "To a pleasant evening and hopefully more to come."

Paige seemed caught off guard by his open demeanor and for a brief moment Alec saw beyond her façade. Even though she was outwardly cool and confident, he detected a wounded soul inside.

Taking a draught of his whisky, Alec asked Paige what fed her spirit and engaged her mind. Was she a planner, a doer, or go-getter? Did she value people, possessions, or ideas? Alec thoroughly enjoyed their conversation. Paige responded to all his questions thoughtfully, and he shared facets of his personality with her as well. Without meaning to, Alec found himself deeply attracted to Paige Anderson.

He explained that he was a Leo and pretty true to his sign. He basically had a sunny outlook on life and a flair for the dramatic. Wanting to know whether he guessed her sign, Paige asked, "So, what am I?"

With his eyes sparkling in amusement, Alec spoke his thoughts out loud. "Let's see. You're either a fire sign like me or possibly an air sign. You have a quick wit and, you seem playful and forthright. I think you're either a Sagittarian or an Aquarian. Did I get that right?"

Laughing merrily, Paige answered, "No. I'm an Aries."

With a slightly deflated ego, he responded, "Well, at least I was correct about one thing. You are a fire sign. I'm just glad my income doesn't depend upon my astrological skill."

When that topic was exhausted, Alec told her about his career in banking and his current responsibilities as Liaison Officer. Trusting the subject of murder wouldn't put a damper on their tête-à-tête, Alec explained that he was primarily auditing Linley's books. He didn't want to put her on the defensive.

After a second round of drinks was delivered, Alec tried to think of a tactful way to bring up her past. Absentmindedly, he began to swivel the scotch in his glass.

Reacting to the momentary lapse in conversation, Paige said, "You appear uneasy. Did you want to ask me something?"

Alec took a deep breath and tried his bluff. "Look. I know you served with Mark Linley several years ago. Why didn't you tell the police about it?"

Paige turned ashen for a moment and gazed deeply at Alec, apparently wondering whether she could trust him.

It seemed like an eternity for her to reply. Hesitantly, Paige answered, "I was afraid. I hated Mark and I believed that once the police started to poke around, they'd think that I killed him. He was a petty man who took pleasure in destroying people's lives. Because of him, my brother lost his job in total disgrace.

Up until then, Alec thought Mark Linley was a nuisance and capable of pulling off a scam or two. Observing Paige's anguished expression, Alec started to see him in a more sinister light. Softly he said, "Tell me what happened. I won't repeat it, unless it's vital to the murder investigation."

Paige told Alec the bare facts. She explained that she and her younger brother Derek had worked on the Centaurius with Mark three years ago.

At that time, they were on the Panama Canal winter tour, and Derek was one of the Assistant Food and Beverage managers. Needing to settle a poker debt, Derek stole a jar of malossal caviar from the ship and sold it to a casino in Aruba for two hundred dollars.

With a sob in her voice, Paige said, "A few days before he took the damn thing, Derek asked me for money. Instead of lending it to him, I gave him this big lecture on being more responsible. None of this would have happened if I had just given him the cash."

"Did Linley find out about the theft after conducting an inventory of kitchen foodstuffs?"

Paige nodded miserably. "Mark didn't know who took the caviar at first. Derek admitted to stealing it after being threatened and hounded for weeks. I understand it was Mark's job to report it. But, I'll never forgive him for taking such delight in ending my brother's shipboard career."

As she finished her story, Paige searched Alec's face for his reaction. Trying to hide his anger toward Mark, Alec merely replied, "I can see why you didn't want to tell the police. However Lass, they will find out!"

Sensing her despondency, Alec suggested a walk on the Sun Deck. Paige agreed that she could use some fresh air. While Alec signed for the drinks, he wondered whether it was a smart to go in to the moonlight with her. His Scottish intuition told him she was innocent. Unfortunately, it had been wrong before.

There were only a few passengers on the promenade, as it was quite cool with an occasional strong breeze. Alec gave Paige his cutaway jacket, and they chatted about the stars and constellations. While Alec was pointing out Betelgeuse in Orion's Belt, Paige suddenly turned to face him and declared, "I've been an awful coward. When we return to Florida on Wednesday, I'll tell the homicide detective I had a clash with Mark several years ago."

Alec put his hand on her shoulder and said, "I'm glad. I think it will be better for you in the long run."

She, in turn, rewarded Alec with a smile that lit up her entire face.

It was at that moment that Alec did something he thought he would never do again. He gently placed his hands beside her upturned face and brought his lips down to hers. Softly, then more intensely, he began to explore her mouth. A moan escaped from deep within his soul, and he released her.

Alec whispered hoarsely. "Paige. I'm sorry. I shouldn't have done that."

Paige smiled quizzically and said softly, "I really liked your kiss. I would welcome another one when you're ready."

Alec grinned and replied, "That's a deal." Deciding it would be a good time to end their "date," he accompanied Paige to her cabin.

At the door, she gave him back his coat and thanked him for a wonderful evening. Alec's room was just a little farther down the hall. Too upset to go to sleep, Alec walked past his cabin and headed back to the promenade deck. He wasn't prepared for the depth of passion that Paige had awakened in him. Although Alec hated himself at that moment, he wanted to make love to her.

CHAPTER 5

▼

"TOUCH ME IN THE MORNING"

Words & Music—Michael Masser & Ronald Miller

Wednesday Morning—25th of January

Alec felt guilt-ridden when he woke up the next day. To combat his sense of distress, he decided to concentrate on work. The first task on Alec's agenda was to check his e-mail. He wanted to find out whether the Fort Lauderdale Sheriff's Department had concluded Mark Linley's autopsy and the investigation of the crime scene. More importantly, Alec needed to examine the layout of the fitness center and confront Gwen on several issues. Today he knew a lot more than yesterday.

Just as Alec was preparing to leave his half eaten breakfast on the table, Douglas came up behind him with his tray of food. "Do my eyes deceive me? You didn't finish your meal!" Flinging one more barb at Alec, he added, "You mustn't be feeling well."

Alec grunted. "Oh, go away."

Douglas sat down instead. "I think you'd better come down to my office so that I can run a few tests on you."

Since his good friend seemed determined to stay where he was, Alec asked for a coffee refill from a passing waiter and watched Douglas eat his breakfast. The doctor cut his pancakes as though he were engaged in some delicate surgical procedure. As much as Alec enjoyed his company, he realized Douglas had no passion for food.

After dissecting his sausage, Douglas glanced up at Alec. "So tell me. What happened with Paige?"

Alec stared at his coffee. "She made me feel things, I thought I had buried."

"You didn't tell her, did you?"

"No, I suppose I should. But, I'm not even sure she's interested in me. The whole thing is so bloody uncomfortable!"

Ignoring his tirade, Douglas interposed, "Paige stopped by the infirmary bright and early this morning. She thanked me for introducing you two. Knowing the fairer sex as I do, I think she also wanted to find out if you were married. It's a good thing Maggie interrupted our conversation. What happened last night?"

Alec gave him a few details about their evening. When he mentioned their moonlight walk and subsequent kiss, Douglas choked down a laugh. "So that's why you're so gloomy. You're a silly sod!"

The doctor's reaction jolted Alec back to reality. Was it *that* awful he found Paige attractive? Realizing he was being daft, Alec decided to leave the ball in her court. Feeling much better, Alec rose from his chair.

"So, where are you going?"

Alec looked at Douglas as if he had two heads. "I'll be right back. I'm getting myself a stack of pancakes."

With maple syrup residue on his fingers, Alec headed off to the Internet Den to open his shipboard account. On the way, Alec stopped off at the restroom to wash his hands. It wouldn't do for his fingers to stick to the keyboard. Passengers were charged seventy-five cents per minute to "surf the net." Even with his 40 percent crewmember discount, Alec realized it would still cost a pretty penny. The telephone was even dearer. The Pegasus charged $7.95 per minute for ship-to-shore calls.

Luckily for Alec, the Internet manager was available to help him activate his account. Alec simply gave the young man his room key and created a password to log into the system. To check his incoming messages, Alec clicked on his Internet Service Provider and signed onto its home page. The number of messages in his mail center was staggering. At forty-five cents per minute, Alec felt it was shameful to use good money to delete advertisements.

Out of fifty-seven messages he saved only two—one from his parents and the other from McGill. Since Alec was basically frugal, he printed out both and logged off the computer. He could always get back to them later.

Alec collected his copies and receipt of charges. Eager to read his mail, Alec went into the neighboring library and took a seat in a high-backed wing chair. He read the note from his parents first. Certain they were well, Alec began McGill's e-mail.

Subj: Homicide Investigation
Date: 24th January, 7:42:51 PM EST
From: Dan.McGill@coflso.net
To: AlecDunBarton@aol.com

Here is the update I promised you. The crime scene unit was unable to discover anything substantial in the gym. There were no skin fragments or fingerprints left on the dumbbell, and the capsule contained nothing but Mark Linley's blood and hair. The medical examiner concluded that he died from a cerebral hemorrhage at 5:30 that morning. His toxicology screen showed no abnormalities.

The forensics team was able to isolate several fingerprints in the victim's cabin that belonged to Michelle Van Dam, a massage therapist, who works in your spa. Since I didn't interview her, I want you to find out about their relationship. The location of her prints leads us to believe they were intimate.

I haven't received a reply from your human resources department yet. I hope to have the personnel records of the entire crew faxed to me by Friday. I understand that includes nearly 700 people. Yesterday, we began to review the passenger manifest.

I was able to investigate the backgrounds of the Americans (Rick Tanner, Janet Kane, and Beth Romano) who were present at the victim's last meal. The only one with a record was Tanner with a recent DWI charge.

So far, Linley's computer has revealed nothing in the way of a personal nature. His desk and office were clean of prints, except for his and Scott Harris's.

My partner and I were able to interview Janet Kane this morning at her home in Boca Raton. She has taken your cruise on three separate occasions and spoke to Linley for the first time on Saturday evening. When he left the table, she heard him say the word *model*, not bottle.

Please contact me at your earliest convenience and advise me of your progress.

I was expecting to have more by now.

Dan McGill

Alec's response to the e-mail was "blimey." Several elderly people in the library eyed him, decided he was probably sane, and returned to their reading and trivia games.

The liaison officer's thoughts turned to Paige. It would be just a matter of time before McGill learned of her relationship with Mark. If she agreed, he'd gladly intercede on her behalf. In the meantime, Alec hoped to find some evidence that pointed to other suspects.

Without wasting a minute, Alec headed off to the spa, which was located in the forward section of the Lido Deck. Alec found the title *spa* misleading as it included three different departments: the beauty salon, the massage and treatment rooms, and the fitness center. In order to get to the gym, Alec passed the main reception area. A woman seated at the desk glanced up and asked whether he needed some help. Sounding like a Scottish *Terminator*, Alec smiled and responded, "I'll be back."

Alec was awed by the view in the gym. The entire forward section looked out upon the ocean like a figurehead on an old sailing vessel. Fragrances of eucalyptus and sandalwood assailed his nostrils. It smelled nothing like any fitness center Alec had ever visited.

Along the bank of windows, passengers were using various types of exercise equipment. Behind the treadmills, there was a rack of dumbbells arranged by size and weight. On the other side of the gym, Alec noticed several women seated on floor mats. Aware that Gwen was giving a yoga class, Alec turned to leave.

He didn't get very far before hearing, "Welcome to my world. I'm glad you came up to see me."

As Gwen came forward, Alec gave her an indulgent smile. Playing her game, he said, "I was hoping to get you alone."

Gwen placed her hand on Alec's upper arm and looked into his eyes. "I'm off at two this afternoon. Why don't you come back then? We can sit by the pool. My tan is beginning to fade, and you can help me apply oil to those hard to reach places."

Alec winked. "I'd be delighted."

Ready to see his next "suspect," Alec returned to the reception area. "I'm back," he stated. "I'd like to see Ms. Van Dam."

Checking her appointment book, the receptionist replied, "Michelle has an opening now. She can squeeze you in for a thirty-minute massage."

Alec had the time, but wasn't entirely sure he wanted *her* hands around his neck as he asked indelicate questions. Trying to make up his mind, he inquired, "Do I get a discount?"

The woman shook her head, "Not on sea days. Today, we're running a Half-Body Stress-Away Massage for forty dollars. Normally it's sixty. Even on port days your crew discount would only save you nine dollars."

Alec handed over his room key. Though, he was pleased to be getting a bargain, he had concerns about the term "half-body." When she gave him back his card and sales receipt, Alec asked awkwardly, "What should I wear?"

She smiled at his confusion, "Most men wrap a towel around themselves. Wait here while I prepare the room and get Michelle."

Alec began to have doubts as soon as she left. He didn't want to make a fool of himself during his first professional massage.

The receptionist returned with a plump blond woman who was dressed in a flared, white salon coat. She was the young lady who had approached Alec two nights ago after the captain's meeting. As she greeted him, Alec detected recognition in her eyes.

Michelle accompanied him to a small room that was simply decorated with large posters advertising the spa's health and beauty products. A chair stood in the corner and a massage table occupied the center of the cubicle. Bottles of lotions and creams stood on a nearby cart ready to be used.

The masseuse told Alec to take a seat and explained that the spa required its clients to answer some medical questions. As he took the out-stretched clipboard from her hand, Alec glimpsed at the attached question-naire. Smiling, he said, "I'll answer yours, if you answer mine."

Michelle replied, "I was hoping to get a chance to speak to you. We can talk while I do your back."

She left Alec to complete the form and undress. When she returned, Alec was seated on the table clad in his terry cloth towel. Michele looked over his responses to the questionnaire and inquired about his leg cramps. She then instructed Alec to lie face down on the table.

Michelle warmed some lotion in her palms. Positioning herself at his head, she began to move her hands from the top of his shoulders to the small of his back along his spine. Alec felt blissful. Her hands kneaded his tired skin and muscles with just the right amount of pressure. The lyrics from the song "Touch Me in the Morning" went through Alec's mind. He wondered how upset Michelle had been over Mark's death and whether she was "glad for the time together." Alec needed to speak to her before he forgot the reason he was there.

Clearing his throat, he managed to ask, "What did you want to tell me after the captain's meeting?"

At that prompt, Michelle launched into a ten-minute monologue about her relationship with Mark Linley. Alec learned that Michelle had been secretly dating him for over a year. Even though she was aware that many of Mark's coworkers gave him a wide berth, Michelle felt that he was sensitive and caring. She became more animated as she explained how Mark worried about their sixteen-year age difference. He didn't want *her* to feel uncomfortable, so they spent their evenings exclusively in his cabin.

If Alec hadn't been feeling so groggy, he would have said something out loud. Instead he thought, "That poor deluded child. Did she finally realize she was being used and bludgeon him to death?"

Michelle moved down from his lower back to the backs of his thighs. As she pummeled and kneaded Alec's tight muscles, she finally told him the reason she'd sought him out in the first place. "Mark came here the day before he died, frightened and upset. He said he was going to transfer to another ship because his assistant, Scott Harris, was threatening him."

Alec twisted his head around so that he could see Michelle's expression. "Do you know what Harris said to him?"

Concentrating on a knot in the center of one leg, Michelle replied. "He didn't go into specifics, just that Scott stole crystal, and he wasn't going to get away with it. When I asked him what he planned to do, he gave me this weird look and said he was gonna 'sit on it for a while.'"

As Michelle continued massaging his calves, Alec wondered why Scott Harris would steal glassware. The Pegasus didn't carry lead crystal. Alec couldn't imagine why the controller was murdered over something so petty.

With seconds left in their session, Alec asked, "Were you upset that Mark planned to put in a transfer?"

Michelle frowned. "I was sort of angry with him. He didn't even ask me if I wanted to join him. I called him a selfish bastard. The next day he died, and I felt awful. I never got a chance to apologize."

Before Michele left him to dress, Alec tried to lighten the mood and said, "Don't worry. One day, I think it will all make sense." Alec wasn't sure where that sentiment came from. But he hoped with all his heart, it were true.

Three hours later, Alec was ready for Gwen Llewelyn. After the massage, his body felt like jelly. Although he wanted to take a nap, Alec decided to spend his time going over the ship's inventory of stemware.

The office was deserted when Alec arrived, and he was able to sift through the papers unhampered. At noon, he stopped long enough to pick up a cheeseburger and iced tea from the officer's mess hall.

As the time to meet Gwen approached, Alec realized he'd have to come back later. There was no evidence of missing crystal. Alec replaced the files and went to his cabin to put on a bathing suit.

When Alec arrived at the spa gym, Zack, the male fitness director, showed Alec the dumbbells and exercise equipment while Gwen changed. Alec didn't mind the wait. It gave him an opportunity to snoop. Noticing a white oblong cylinder partially hidden behind a wicker screen, Alec exclaimed, "Is that the Alpha Capsule?"

Zack nodded, as Alec started to walk toward it. He was thrilled to see that the Pegasus had one. He had incorrectly assumed that Detective McGill's forensic unit took away the ship's only machine. Astounded, he asked, "Did you have two?"

At that moment, Gwen appeared and answered for Zack. "No. We picked up this one in Port Everglades. The Monoceros had two."

Alec sat on the edge of the platform. "Can I try it?"

Gwen smiled, "You'll owe me!"

She proceeded to show Alec all its various knobs and buttons. For the music selection, Alec chose Mark's compact disc of whale and ocean songs.

As he settled into the capsule, Alec said, "Lass, I'd like you to do me a favor."

Gwen shook her head and acknowledged she understood his instructions.

Alec closed the lid over his body. He then adjusted the volume on the headphones, shut his eyes, and tried to get acclimated to the different sensations. After a minute or two passed, Alec began to wonder about Gwen's whereabouts. He opened his eyes just in time to see a ten-pound weight hurling toward him.

Thank God, Gwen had the physical control to stop the weight before it hit Alec's skull. Standing over his body, she shouted eagerly, "Did I do it right?"

Alec turned off the machine and replied in a slightly shaky voice, "Yes. It was perfect."

Before carrying out his little experiment, Alec felt sure that Linley would have heard a sound or felt a rush of air, alerting him to the killer's presence. He now knew that the music, the steady hum of the machine, and the constant spray of aromatic herbs, made it impossible to detect anyone's approach.

Energized by this knowledge, Alec was ready for a swim. Gwen quickly retrieved her tote bag from the back room and tugged on Alec's arm. "Let's go," she urged. "I want to go to the pool on the Riviera Deck. It shouldn't be crowded there."

At the pool, Gwen arranged two deck chairs to directly face the sun while Alec took a couple of towels from the supply rack. On his return, she removed her swimsuit cover up and stretched out seductively on the lounge. Gwen was dressed or practically undressed in a purple two-piece bikini.

After his brush with death, Alec was ready for a drink. He wanted a Scotch, but suspected it would impede his finely-honed sleuthing skills.

Gwen patted the chair beside her.

Not ready to sit, Alec said, "Can I get you a beverage before I do your bidding."

Squinting up at him, she replied, "Hmm. I'd love a diet cola with lemon."

Alec smiled inwardly as he thought about the women he had met in the last few days. Michelle was a confused kid, Paige appeared distant and unapproachable until you saw past her mask, and Gwen was a cross between a child and a vamp.

When Alec came back, he had two sodas with him. After placing them on a table next to her lounge chair, he debated whether to cool off first. Coming from Great Britain, he wasn't used to the sun or the heat.

Alec began to remove his shirt and shorts a little self-consciously. He really needed to knock off twenty pounds.

Gwen sipped her drink as she watched Alec undress. "Are you going for a swim?" she whined. "I want you to do my back."

Resignedly, Alec took the chair beside Gwen's. He noticed that she had two bottles of Cruisin' Coconut suntan oil by her feet, and asked, "Which bottle of lotion do you want?"

As she turned on her stomach, she replied, "Use the one that's almost finished. They're both the same."

Alec held them up to the light and took the one that was nearly empty. He twisted off the cap and sniffed the oil appreciatively. It smelled like coconut custard pie.

While he rubbed it on her back and legs, she moaned gently. Gwen seemed very transparent to him. But, he supposed there were lots of men who fell for her act.

With his chores done, Alec walked over to the pool. The sun-drenched cement burned the soles of his feet. At the pool's edge, Alec sat down and let his legs dangle in the clear aqua blue water. Feeling like a malingerer, he thought, "There'll be plenty of time to talk to Gwen later." For now, he just wanted to enjoy the day.

Suddenly, Alec felt two hands on the center of his back about to push him into the pool. Alec turned around swiftly, ready to snap at Gwen. When he saw it was Paige and heard, "Are Leos afraid to get wet," he laughed instead.

As Paige placed her sunglasses on a table, Alec noticed how alluring she looked in her one-piece navy swimsuit. The neckline plunged almost to her navel. For a brief moment, Alec wondered how her breasts stayed inside. Thinking like his so-called twin, James Bond, he then contemplated how he could get them out.

Sliding into the tepid water, he called, "Come join me." Paige used the stepladder to enter the pool. This time, Alec got a lovely view of her shapely back and legs.

Deciding his present train of thought was dangerous, Alec told Paige about the detective's e-mail. Paige listened intently and agreed that Alec should tell McGill about her relationship with Mark Linley. With that out of the way, an uncomfortable moment of silence followed.

Finally, Alec stammered out, "Look, I need to talk to you about last night."

Smiling, she simply said, "Okay."

Just then, Alec saw Gwen approaching the pool. Hurriedly, he asked, "Can we meet this evening?"

Gwen got there just as Paige repeated, "The Lido Bar at 9:00."

For the next twenty minutes they all talked and padded around the water. Gwen told Paige about their experiment in the gym, and Alec detected concern in Paige's voice when she asked whether it could have been dangerous.

As the women conversed, Alec learned about St. Maarten, their first port-of-call. The ship was supposed to dock on the Dutch side by seven A.M. Gwen mentioned that she wanted to get an early start shopping in the French capital city of Marigot.

Seeing Alec's puzzled expression, Paige enlightened him, explaining that the island was the smallest territory in the world governed by two sovereign nations. Alec had never been to the ports on this itinerary and would have liked to go ashore. Sadly, he decided his time would be better spent sorting through financial records. He *needed* to gather more information before responding to McGill's e-mail.

Paige couldn't stay long. She excused herself at three to get ready for a seminar she was giving in the movie theatre. Her topic was "Flagship Cruise Lines' Exotic 180-Day World Cruise."

Gwen appeared happy to get Alec back to herself and dragged him out of the pool. She readjusted the position of their deck chairs, obviously hoping for an intimate conversion. Before she could reach for his hand, Alec bluntly said, "What was going on between you and Mark Linley?"

Gwen looked off in the distance as though she was trying to decide on a tactic. Alec was hoping for the truth. The massage and the sun had knocked him out, and he just wanted to return to his cabin for a shower and nap.

Wearily, he entreated, "Please be honest with me."

After a moment's hesitation, Gwen confirmed Alec's suspicions. She allowed Mark to blackmail her. Since the Southern Dreams' cruise attracted elderly passengers who weren't interested in paying additional fitness fees, she often had trouble meeting her goals. At first the controller said he understood, but later, he suggested a deal. In exchange for the key to the spa, he promised to lower her monetary targets.

After two months, Gwen wanted out. She had become increasingly worried that Zack would catch Mark on the machine. Brian, her former coworker, had known about the arrangement and didn't care. But Zack was a straight arrow. On the morning Gwen found Mark's body in the capsule, she assumed he was asleep. It was only when she noticed all the blood, she realized he was dead.

Alec gazed at her face and felt sure she was telling the truth. Curious about one more thing, Alec inquired, "How did you know that Paige disliked Linley?"

Gwen replied candidly. "A few weeks ago, I saw her watching Mark as he was rummaging through those bottles over there." Gwen pointed to the liquor on display at the Riviera Bar. "Under her breath, I heard her call him an annoying little insect."

Thankful for the facts, Alec fondly patted her shoulder and put on his shirt.

Gwen seemed initially relieved, and then concern for her job overshadowed her mood. "Will you be telling Captain Jarvis or Officer Bauer?"

Alec replied. "I don't plan to. The homicide detective will be informed, but I suspect he'll keep that to himself unless it's crucial to the murder investigation. Don't worry. If it comes up, I'll help you deal with it."

As Alec made his way to his cabin, he admitted to himself that he'd make a terrible cop. Women got to him…one redhead in particular.

CHAPTER 6

▼

"THEY CAN'T TAKE THAT AWAY FROM ME"

Words & Music—George Gershwin & Ira Gershwin

Wednesday Afternoon—25th *of January*

Alec woke up from his nap feeling groggy. When he glanced at the alarm clock to check the time, he noticed that his wet bathing suit was still on the floor. Since Alec fell asleep without a stitch of clothes on, he was thankful that Widi hadn't come in. The poor man would have received quite a shock.

As Alec sat up in bed, he began to review his plans for the evening. Not having found evidence of missing crystal earlier, Alec decided to return to the office after dinner to go through Scott's requisition orders and invoices. Alec was skeptical about what he'd find. The murder occurred three days ago, and Scott had had ample opportunity to cover his tracks.

At nine, Alec had a date with Paige in the Lido Bar. This lounge was located between the buffet restaurant and spa. Alec was very eager to try this hot spot. In the evening, cigar and pipe smokers were permitted to light up. The room had a retractable roof, so its occupants could breathe fresh air and gaze at the starry night.

With his stomach grumbling, Alec dashed into the shower. The hot water stung the back of his neck, and Alec realized he was sunburned. Confident that the doctor had some kind of magic potion, Alec threw on his clothes and hurried along to the infirmary. Douglas had visiting hours till 6:00 P.M.

This time the infirmary door was wide open, and Maggie Hart wasn't standing guard. Instead, Alec saw a dark-haired woman in a nurse's uniform talking to Douglas. After listening to their conversation, Alec guessed that the young lady was Beth Romano. Only Americans pronounced *tomato* like *potato*. She was telling the doctor how to make her mother's tomato sauce from scratch. Beth was wasting her breath. Douglas couldn't tell the difference between homemade and jarred.

Alec stepped in and said, "Hmm. Can I get some service here?"

Douglas turned around to face Alec. "Beth, let me introduce you to my rude friend, Alec DunBarton."

Alec extended his hand to Beth. "I'm glad to meet you."

Deciding that there was no time like the present, he added, "Would you mind if I asked you a few questions now? I'd like to know about the night that you and Dr. Abbot had dinner with Mark Linley."

Beth looked at the doctor slightly alarmed. Douglas smiled encouragingly and said, "Don't worry, he won't bite. He's really quite nice."

In the doctor's office, Alec arranged the chairs so that he and Beth could face each other. Once they were comfortably seated, he gently asked, "Can you remember anything unusual about that night?"

Looking down at her hands, Beth said, "I really didn't know him very well. I tried to steer clear of him after he argued with Nora about those tongue depressors."

Alec acknowledged her statement with a nod of his head. "I'm more interested in your observations and impressions. I understand you heard Mark Linley arguing with the assistant controller when you arrived. What did he say?"

Beth screwed up her face in thought. "They stopped talking when they realized we were going to sit with them. But, I did hear Mark tell Scott not to threaten him."

"Do you remember at what point in the conversation Mark got up to leave?"

Beth started to recite the events out loud, trying to recall the moment. "He sat with us for a while. After Dr. Abbot, Gwen and I joined them, Rick Tanner came over to our table and introduced us to Miss Kane, his fiancée. About fifteen minutes later, Janet went to the ladies' room and when she returned, Mark asked her where she purchased her handbag. She told him she bought it at Bloomingdale's, and he gave her this weird smile and said it was 'one of a kind.' The conversation was pretty strange, even for Mark. He left after that."

"Did Mark say anything when he walked away?"

"The police asked me the same question. As he passed me, I thought I heard him mention the word *bottle*."

Thinking about McGill's e-mail, Alec followed up. "Is it possible that Janet heard *model* instead?"

Beth shook her head indecisively. "I don't know. At that time, she had been showing me her engagement ring—a huge marquise-cut diamond with baguettes on the sides. I never saw anything so beautiful!"

Alec smiled at Beth's enthusiasm and asked his final question. "What happened after Linley left the table?"

"Janet and Rick told us about their plans to marry in Barbados in April. Scott gave them lots of information about the island. He said that his family came from there originally. Dr. Abbot never took his eyes off Janet, and Gwen hardly said a word. She seemed really miserable. Later on, I caught her giving Rick's girlfriend the finger."

As they walked to the outer office, Alec chuckled to himself visualizing Gwen with her nemesis.

On seeing Beth and Alec approach, Douglas asked, "Are you finished pestering my nurse?"

Alec smiled sweetly and said, "No. I actually came here because I'm in dire need of medical attention."

Douglas gave Alec the once over. "You have some sunburn! Haven't you ever heard of sunscreen?"

"Listen, I didn't come here to be ridiculed. Give me something for the pain and let's go eat. I'm starved."

Beth giggled in the background as she took a tube of first aid cream from a drawer. She handed it to Douglas, and Douglas handed it to Alec. With Alec's condition diagnosed and medication prescribed, the two men headed off to supper.

The Lido Restaurant was serving Italian dishes along with long loaves of bread and assorted antipasto. Alec made a beeline for cheese-encrusted lasagna, while Douglas took a bowl of rather plain spaghetti and three small meatballs. The air outside was still too hot, so the men took seats at one of the last inside tables.

Just as Alec asked Douglas about his day, a familiar looking young man came over to their table. He nodded to Alec and said, "Dr. Abbot, may I join you and your companion?"

Douglas smiled and pulled out the chair as the man lowered his tray onto the table. "I'm not sure if you've met our Liaison Officer yet. This is Alec DunBarton. Alec, this is Boyd Griffin, our saxophonist extraordinaire."

On hearing the introduction, Alec realized he was Gwen's on and off boyfriend, and one of the musicians who played last night at the Zodiac Bar. While Douglas chatted with him, Alec gave him the once over. He was a perfect specimen, well over six feet tall without an inch of fat. Alec could understand why Douglas thought he and Gwen made a handsome pair.

Douglas voiced what was on Alec's mind. "No Gwen tonight?"

Swallowing a piece of garlic bread, he replied, "Uh uh. She decided to work one of Zack's shifts so she could go into St. Maarten tomorrow."

From his tone, it appeared that Boyd and Gwen were back together. Alec found himself wondering *when* it happened and *if* Miss Llewelyn would be less flirtatious with her steady beau at hand.

Boyd couldn't stay long. He explained to Alec that he usually performed at one of the four lounges every evening from 7:15 to 8:15 for the second-seating cocktail hour. Tonight he was playing in the Constellation Lounge.

After Boyd left, Douglas asked, "Have you gotten to that bar yet?"

Alec shook his head, and Douglas went on to describe the room. "The lounge is incredible. It's on the Sun Deck and totally enclosed by glass. At dusk, you can watch the sun set. Once it becomes dark, small bright lights in the domed ceiling sparkle in the configuration of constellations." Winking, he added, "It's very romantic. You should go there with Paige."

Alec grunted at that remark. "I'm meeting her later tonight to tell her about Shanna and Emma. It hurts like blazes just mentioning their names."

Douglas gave his friend a sympathetic look. "I can't begin to understand what you're going through. But, I do think it will be good for you to talk about it."

To change the subject, Alec asked Douglas about his nurses. He couldn't seem to remember which one was which. The doctor explained that Beth was single, in her early twenties, and from Philadelphia. Nora, on the other hand, was married to one of the ships' plumbers, in her thirties, and raised in Liverpool. Hearing the two described so succinctly, Alec expected he wouldn't mix them up.

Over coffee, Alec and Douglas made plans to meet the following evening for drinks in the Constellation Bar. Since passengers usually returned from their first port-of-call with ailments ranging from heat exhaustion to foot blisters, Douglas thought he might be late. Alec told him he'd have no trouble starting without him. As he headed toward his office, Alec realized he was becoming a lounge lizard.

Alec had a productive evening. After rummaging through dirty invoices in his office, he found a vital piece of evidence by sheer good fortune. Just as he was locking the outside door Scott arrived. He looked slightly alarmed at meeting Alec and said he was planning to work late to catch up on some reports.

Though Alec would have liked to question him then and there, he didn't want to keep Paige waiting. Instead he asked, "Do you think we could meet sometime tomorrow and put our heads together?"

"I'll be in the office all morning," Scott replied. "Is ten all right with you?"

Alec amiably agreed. Taking the elevator to the Lido Deck, Alec deemed, "Let the man have one more good night's sleep."

A tropical breeze welcomed Alec as he stepped into the open-deck lounge. The bar's rattan furniture consisted of couches, chairs, and coffee tables that could easily be rearranged to accommodate different-sized groups. The brightly colored chair and sofa cushions made the area appear informal and cozy. Before Alec took a seat on one of the couches that faced the starlit sky, he removed his pipe and tobacco pouch from his pants pockets and placed them on an end table. If the evening ended badly, at least he'd get a chance to smoke.

Alec didn't have to wait long for Paige. She seemed to come from nowhere and sat down on the chair adjacent to the couch.

Slightly out of breath, she asked, "Have you been here long?"

This was the first time Alec had seen her in her uniform. Even in a plain white skirt and blouse, she was eye-catching. Paige wanted her usual gin and tonic with lime and Alec his Scotch. After placing the orders at the bar, Alec returned to find Paige mischievously playing with the Velcro clasp on his tobacco pouch.

Caught in the act, she grinned. "I didn't know you smoked. My dad has a pipe like Sherlock Holmes. The smell of tobacco always brings back happy memories."

"Tonight I brought my almond blend," grinned Alec.

A few seconds later, the waiter served their drinks, along with a dish of salted nuts. Too preoccupied to make a toast, Alec took a gulp of his whisky. More to himself, than Paige, he muttered, "I need to get this off my chest."

As Alec took another mouthful, Paige interjected, "You're not married or gay, are you?"

Alec smiled for a second, and then his face took on a look of despair.

Paige moved beside him on the couch.

Grasping her hand tightly, Alec slowly began to tell her about Shanna, his wife, and Emma, their four-year-old daughter. During the next few minutes, Paige heard about Alec's marriage, his life in London, and his plans for the future.

Searching for the words, Alec simply explained, "Six months ago, my wife and child were killed. A drunk driver hit them as they were walking to Harrods Department Store on Knightsbridge Road. Everything I was and would ever be died that day."

Softly, Paige asked, "What happened to the driver?"

Realizing he was crushing Paige's fingers, Alec let go of her hand. He downed his Scotch in one swallow and signaled the bartender for another round of drinks. With a cold edge to his voice, he continued. "Days later, the man died from internal injuries. I never got a chance to confront him or my anger.

"I still blame myself. Shanna and I had words that morning. She wanted me to spend the day with them. Instead, I watched a bloody cricket match on television. If I had been there, I might have been able to prevent their deaths. I think it's the real reason, I feel honor bound to catch Linley's killer. Maybe then, I'll be able to regain a sense of control over my life."

Paige nodded. Her face clouded with sadness and remorse.

Seeing her expression, Alec gently added, "Lass, I didn't want to depress you, but I thought you should know. Before coming on this ship, I convinced myself that I would never meet another woman. You've awoken emotions in me that were dormant. I don't want to let go of those feelings, and I don't want to lead you on. Do I make any sense?"

"I think you're telling me that you'd like to *see* me, but you can't make any promises." Paige stopped speaking while the waiter set down fresh drinks.

When they were alone again, she continued. "I haven't had anyone in my life for a long time. I would like to get to know you better."

Alec exhaled, feeling relieved. His instinct was to put his arms around Paige, but he lifted his glass instead. "To you and to life."

Exploring a "safer" subject, Paige and Alec discussed the murder for the next hour. Alec hadn't any proof that Paige was innocent, but he didn't and wouldn't consider her a suspect. He told her about the investigation and felt no compunction about sharing his thoughts as well.

By their third drink, they were companionably silent. Seated on the couch, Alec serenely puffed on his pipe while Paige rested her head against his chest. With his free arm, he held her closely.

Alec wished that time would stand still, but the waiters had other ideas. They had begun to collect the glasses and put away the seat cushions. Taking the cue, Alec walked Paige to her cabin. At the door, they made a date to meet for breakfast.

Hesitant to disturb the magical quality of their evening, Alec paused a moment before reaching out to her. Unable to stop the torrent of emotions that had been welling up inside, Alec swept her in his arms and kissed her passionately. As their bodies pressed close together, Alec felt those familiar stirrings. Although he yearned for further contact, he released her and watched her slip into her stateroom.

The next morning, Alec woke up thinking of Shanna. For the first time since she'd died, he was able to think of her without pain. Somewhere from the back of his mind came the lyrics to "They Can't Take That Away From Me." As Alec hummed the Gershwin tune, he acknowledged that Shanna would always haunt his dreams. But, "The memory of all that" wouldn't always hurt.

As Alec prepared to meet Paige at eight thirty, he felt apprehensive, fearing that she changed her mind during the night. His relief was considerable when he approached the Lido Restaurant and saw her waiting for him with a warm smile.

Once they were seated, Paige told him about her family in Palo Alto, California, her college days, and her failed marriage. She explained that she often found it difficult to get close to people. He learned that Paige's mother died of breast cancer when she was just nine years old. Her father, an elementary school principal, struggled alone to raise her and Derek. Alec gathered from Paige's remarks that she'd had a rough childhood.

At 9:50, the announcement for Snowball Jackpot Bingo served to remind Alec and Paige of the time. They had ten minutes to get to their allotted appointments. Before parting at the elevator, Paige tilted her head up for a kiss, and Alec made sure she went away satisfied.

Alec walked to his office ready for an accounting duel of wits. Scott was seated at his computer, drinking a cup of tea when Alec entered. The assistant controller smiled congenially, and Alec wondered how long that would last.

Once they settled themselves at Alec's desk, Scott inquired, "How can I assist you?"

Carefully, Alec removed a small piece of paper from his shirt pocket. Before showing it to Scott, he said, "I found this rather interesting invoice last night."

Scott took the paper from Alec and opened it quickly. Suddenly looking sick, Scott gasped, "You know!"

"Do you have anything to say for yourself?"

Scott shook his head. "It's too late to pretend. Mark had been holding this over me for weeks. If I hadn't known about his early morning sessions in that Alpha Capsule, he would have exposed me immediately. After he died, I turned the office upside down searching for this champagne invoice. Where was it?"

"I discovered it by accident. Every time I sat at Mark's desk, I banged my knees. Yesterday, I had quite enough with the damn chair and lowered the height of the seat. I found the sales receipt wedged between the chair cushion and wood backing. Just how long have you been stealing Roederer *Cristal* Brut from the ship's stores?"

Scott looked wretched. "I'll tell you everything you want to know. But you've got to believe me. I didn't kill Mark. I was with a friend when he was murdered."

Since the medical examiner placed Mark's death at five thirty in the morning, Alec deduced that Scott had an overnight guest. He tried to get her name tactfully.

Scott nervously tapped his pencil on the edge of the desk, appearing reluctant to hand over the information. After a few seconds of obvious discomfort, he blurted out, "I spent the evening with Eric Santos, the port and shopping specialist. I don't want him to get into any trouble. He knows nothing of my extracurricular activities."

At that moment, it became clear to Alec that the Pegasus was like a television soap opera. Even though Scott's sexual preference probably had no bearing on the case, it suggested there might be other surprising relationships among the crew.

Alec decided to table that thought for the time being. Right now, he wanted to know how Scott managed to steal over $10,000 worth of champagne. Alec didn't have to work too hard to get the information.

His spirit broken, Scott explained how his scheme worked. As the assistant controller, he sent out requisitions for wine and liquor. Instead of ordering 15 six-bottle cases of Roederer Cristal Brut Rose every three months, he ordered 20 cases. When the champagne was delivered, Scott would keep five cases for himself. He would then adjust the computer invoice to corporate headquarters to reflect a higher price per bottle from $235.00 to $280.00. Only connoisseurs of fine wines would know that they were being overcharged.

"How did Linley find out?" queried Alec.

Scott began to show more animation as he answered. "The hardest part was getting the champagne off the ship. I sold it in Barbados, but I could take only one case at a time. About two months ago Mark saw me going ashore with a rectangular-shaped duffle. It wasn't until he found a case of champagne hidden in a storage closet that he became suspicious of me. After checking my invoices, he learned the truth."

Alec was pleased by his confession. He caught an embezzler who knew all about Linley's visits to the fitness center. Scott had a motive to kill him, and he was certainly strong enough to crush his skull with a ten-pound weight.

But, Alec wondered. Was Scott Harris capable of cold-blooded murder?

CHAPTER 7

▼

"SWEET TALKIN' GUY"

Words & Music—Doug Morris, Elliot Greenberg, Barbara Baer,
and Robert Schwartz

Thursday Afternoon—26th of January

Alec's morning ended on a high note. After Scott Harris confessed, Alec paged Captain Jarvis and Officer Bauer. The two men arrived within minutes of each other.

Once the captain fully understood the intricacies of Harris's embezzlement scheme, he relieved Scott of duty and placed him under "house arrest" for the duration of the cruise. The security chief escorted him to his cabin, where he was to remain until the lawyers at headquarters decided upon an appropriate course of action. As an additional security measure, Harris's passport was confiscated.

Before heading back to the bridge, Jarvis asked Alec to contact McGill to let him know about Scott's incarceration. He, in turn, planned to notify his superiors and arrange for a new assistant controller.

After a well-earned lunch and rest, Alec decided to have a word with Eric Santos. He didn't want to e-mail McGill before confirming Scott's alibi.

In order to locate the port and shopping specialist, Alec obtained a daily program of events from the front desk. According to the timetable, Eric was scheduled to discuss "Bargains in Barbados" at 4:00 P.M. Since it was just three, Alec sought out Paige.

The future-cruise desk was located in a corner of a sitting area on the Lower Promenade Deck, directly below the atrium. From the grand staircase, Alec could see Paige with a passenger. Expecting her to finish soon, Alec waited.

Since Paige didn't see him approach, her expression was one of surprise when a gentleman with a Scottish accent whispered in her ear, "Lass, I have an overwhelming urge to be with you. Can you take a break now?"

Paige smiled, locked her desk, and took Alec's arm. "Where to?"

Ready for refreshments, they walked up a flight of stairs to the Churchill Room for afternoon tea. Although the room was filling up, they were able to find a corner table toward the rear. Alec found Paige's radiant face far preferable to Bauer's pale one. This time, Alec showed more restraint in serving himself. He took three little sandwiches and two desserts.

Once they were served their tea, Alec told Paige about Scott's confession and arrest. Apprehensive for his welfare, Paige exclaimed, "Wasn't that dangerous? You didn't know at the time he had an alibi. He could have attacked you!"

Alec grinned. It was rather hard for him to imagine Scott coming at him with blood lust. Thinking of the other kind of lust, Alec asked, "What would you like to do tomorrow night, milady?"

Paige looked into his eyes and replied, "There's going to be a 1950's Beach Party on the Lido Deck. They'll be serving barbequed food around the pool and playing music under the stars. Would you like to dance the slow numbers with me?"

Eager to feel her warm body next to his, he responded, "I can't think of anything I'd like better. When should I collect you?"

"Hesitating over the time, she replied, "I think we should make it later than earlier. I have to deliver some cruise brochures in Barbados and meet with guests at the Crane Beach Resort."

Paige went on to explain that Flagship Cruises had affiliations with four-star hotels throughout the Caribbean. Since she didn't expect to return until five, and wanted to shower and dress before dinner, Alec promised to come for her at 6:30.

All too soon teatime ended and the two parted halfheartedly. As Alec started walking toward the Starlight Lounge, he realized he never seemed to get enough of her. He knew he wouldn't feel content until their bodies clung together after making love.

Alec arrived at the Starlight Lounge to find Eric Santos midway through his discussion of Bridgetown. Preferring not to be seen, he took a seat in the back. Alec's attention wandered while Eric talked about the shops that were recommended by the cruise line.

As Eric distributed shopping coupons, Alec scrutinized the man. Like Harris, he was immaculately groomed and appeared to be in his mid fifties.

Eric's lecture ended several minutes later. At its conclusion, a few passengers gathered around him. Alec waited in the background while a middle-aged woman asked him where she could purchase Barbadian rum at a discounted price. When she departed, Eric glared at Alec and said, "I suppose you're here about Scott."

Alec was surprised that Santos had heard about his arrest and assumed that the ship's grapevine was responsible. Showing no emotion, Alec nodded and said, "Why don't we sit awhile? I have some questions."

"I prefer to stand. Just ask them and go."

Tersely, Alec inquired, "How did you find out about his arrest?"

Looking irritated, Eric responded, "Scott called me from his cabin a few hours ago."

It didn't occur to Alec to ask Bauer to disconnect his phone. Guessing Scott told Eric what to say, Alec asked without conviction, "Were you with the assistant controller on the morning of the 22nd?"

Eric's voice rose an octave. "Look, we were together. But, I'm sorry I ever got involved with him. No one on this ship knows I'm gay, and I'd like to keep it that way. Can you keep my name out of it?"

Hoping for cooperation, Alec said he would try, but couldn't make any promises. "When did you leave Scott's room?"

More cordially, Eric replied. "I left later than I planned. I wanted to avoid Widarta. He's such a busybody and notices everything. Unfortunately, that morning we both overslept until seven. I think the cabin boy saw me slip out."

Satisfied, Alec departed. Eric Santos appeared far too selfish to cover up for Scott Harris.

Alec's next stop was the officer's lounge to respond to the detective's e-mail. Concern about what and how much to say weighed on his mind. Alec felt obligated to tell McGill about Paige, but also wanted to minimize her involvement. After some soul searching, Alec fairly recounted *all* the information he had gathered.

Simply, Alec's e-mail stated that Paige had worked with Mark on the Centaurius three years ago and disliked him, Gwen was increasingly unhappy with Mark's use of the Alpha Capsule, Michelle might have come to realize that she was being used, and Scott—with or without an alibi—had been caught with his proverbial hand in the cookie jar.

After rereading what he wrote, Alec pressed the send icon on the computer and experienced a great sense of relief. To him, Paige sounded the least culpable.

Just as he was about to head out the door, Rick Tanner walked in. Not one to miss an opportunity, Alec remarked, "I was hoping to run into you." Unsure whether the cruise director knew he was helping the police with their inquiries, Alec filled him in and asked, "Would you have time to answer a couple of questions now?"

Rick glanced at his watch. "Unless you talk fast, I think we'd better make it another time. I have a dinner appointment at 6:30."

Alec didn't want to rush with Rick. He also wanted to have a good look at his personal sales checks, and the goals of his staff and department before sitting down with him. Deciding to set a later date, he persisted, "How about tomorrow?"

"I'm spending the day in Barbados. My fiancée wants me to book a resort in Holetown for our wedding reception. I'll be free Saturday."

Alec wasn't sure whether Rick was really busy or just being contrary. In any event, they made arrangements to meet the following day at 4:00 P.M. in the Bull Dog Pub.

Since it was getting rather late, Alec decided to shower, grab a bite, and wait for Douglas in the Constellation Lounge. While he prepared for the evening, Alec wondered why he disliked Tanner. Since the death of his wife and little girl, he had come to despise drunk drivers. However, Alec hadn't known about his DWI when he first saw him in the Starlight Lounge. It then occurred to him that Mark might have been referring to Rick's drinking habits at the "last supper" when he mumbled the word *bottle*. The controller was not above using information of that kind to blackmail others.

The Constellation Lounge lived up to the praise that Douglas had lavished upon it. As the sun had already set when Alec arrived, he decided to return another time with Paige to watch nature at work. The scene was probably breathtaking.

Alec always searched for the perfect place to sit and tonight was no exception. He wanted his back to a wall so he could watch the changing lights of the constellations. Every few minutes the domed ceiling revealed a different view of the stars according to the season. It reminded him of the shows he had seen at the London Planetarium.

After Alec ordered his Glenlivet, he started to tap his feet to the big-band music. Gazing at the band, Alec noticed Boyd on stage. As he listened to him play his sax, Alec concluded he was a gifted musician.

Though this lounge seemed much livelier than the others, Alec acknowledged it was also the first time he was attending a pre-dinner cocktail hour for those passengers who had the late dinner seating.

When the band played "In the Mood," Alec was astonished to see the number of elderly passengers who got up to dance. No matter their age or size, the couples moved with energy and grace. Without warning, a sharp sense of loss overwhelmed Alec. He realized for hundredth time, he would never grow old with Shanna and see their Emma become a woman. Deep in thought, Alec sipped his Scotch and waited for the pain to pass.

Just as the group was wrapping up its last number, Alec spotted Douglas enter the lounge with a young couple. The woman, attired in a white uniform, appeared to be Nora Sheffield, Douglas's second nurse. Alec assumed the man to be her husband Jeffrey, one of the ships' plumbers.

Douglas brought them over to the table. Turning to Alec, he remarked, "I found these waifs wandering around the Sun Deck and thought they might want to take part in some scintillating repartee."

Alec smiled at them and replied, "Oh please join us. Douglas needs to practice. His witty comebacks have been taking awhile to come back."

Not quite speechless, Douglas made the introductions and ordered a round of drinks for everyone.

Once they were served, Alec asked Jeffrey about the duties of a ship's plumber. Jeffrey was happy to oblige and explained that the toilets on the ship work on a vacuum system. If anything, other than toilet paper, was flushed into the tank, a blockage would occur. Jeffrey entertained them with stories about the kinds of items that were discovered in the pipes. Alec's cheeks soon began to hurt from laughing so much.

Becoming pensive for a moment, Alec inquired, "Do you keep a log of the toilets that break down?"

"We do better than that," replied Jeffrey. "Since we've found valuable objects in the system, we also record the reason for the blockage. What do you have in mind?"

In order to explain, Alec told Nora and Jeffrey how Mark Linley met his death. After they digested that information, Alec turned his attention to Jeffrey and asked, "Can you find out which toilets broke down on the 22nd? It's possible our killer didn't consider the plumbing when he or she disposed of evidence."

Speaking more to himself, Alec added, "McGill said the dumbbell was wiped clean of blood and debris. It would be grand if you found something in the works that pointed to the culprit."

Eager to be useful, Jeffrey promised to give Alec a copy of the plumbing repair log within the next few days.

Alec was also interested in the kinds of rumors that circulated among the staff. For the next hour, Nora and Jeffrey came up with several that

Alec knew to be true, and some he just found fascinating. Apparently everyone knew that Scott and Eric were gay, and Gwen was a notorious flirt. Then Nora added, "Rick Tanner is a real sweet talking guy on the make for a rich wife."

As soon as she said *sweet talking guy*, Alec began to sing "Sweeter than sugar, kisses like wine. Don't let him under your skin, cause you'll never win." Recognizing the Chiffon's golden oldie, Jeffrey and Nora joined Alec, "He's a sweet talkin', sweet talkin', sweet talking, sweet talkin' guy."

Douglas rolled his eyes, indicating that Alec was corrupting his friends. Alec, in turn, wondered why Rick needed money when his family was supposed to be loaded.

Alec spent the following morning examining Rick Tanner's financial records. He learned that the cruise director continuously met his goals and had a first-rate staff. His team was responsible for arranging games and trivia contests, organizing sporting events, teaching arts and crafts, coordinating the children's program, and conducting one of the Pegasus's biggest money makers: bingo.

Rick's personal spending seemed a bit high, but not outlandish. He spent little on ship's services, more on drinks, and quite a bit on cash advances. To Alec there was just one reason to use cash on a ship and that was to gamble. If Tanner gambled to excess, it would explain why he needed a rich wife. His parents probably cut him off years ago.

Since the casino was closed and would not reopen until the ship was back in international waters sometime after 10:00 P.M., Alec decided to question the casino staff tomorrow. Having nothing to do for the rest of the afternoon, Alec returned to his cabin to change.

Thirty minutes later, he was comfortably resting on a deck chair near the fresh-water pool on the Lido Deck. The pool area was rather empty, and Alec suspected that many of the passengers were in Bridgetown. Partially obeying the doctor's instructions, Alec applied a sunscreen with an SPF of 7. He bravely rubbed it on his skin despite its texture and odor. His lotion didn't smell like coconut custard pie.

Alec enjoyed the time to himself. He sipped lemonade and watched the waiters set up the buffet tables and decorations for the cookout. Although the ship was docked in the harbor, a gentle breeze played across his body. Not before long Alec was asleep like a "wee bairn." He woke up an hour later to find a waiter looking down at him. Politely, the young man asked Alec whether he'd mind moving to a more isolated place. All the other lounge chairs had been cleared away and the deck party was about to begin.

At 6:30 on the dot, Alec knocked on Paige's door. Paige greeted him in a tropical beach sarong that exposed one shoulder. The colors in her dress brought out her green eyes and coppery-red hair. Seductively, she said, "Would you like to come in for a moment?"

Moved by the sight of her, Alec said. "I may find it difficult to leave."

Undaunted, Paige opened the door wider.

Alec stepped inside and pulled her into his arms. At first, he kissed her lips softy, but soon his hunger for her grew. He began to explore her perfumed neck and shoulders with his mouth.

Paige moaned as she responded to his advances. Fearing he wasn't going too fast, without thought to the consequences, Alec pulled away and apologized. "I'm sorry Lass. I don't want to rush you. It's just that I haven't been with anyone since Shanna. Are you okay?"

Though Paige's expression said it all, she replied, "Mr. DunBarton, I find you irresistible. I may be forced to place *you* under house arrest if you kiss me like that again. We'd better get going now. I'm getting hungry."

The party had been underway for about an hour when they arrived and many of the tables were occupied. In order to hold their spot, Alec waited while Paige went to the buffet. On her return, Alec eyed her food and proceeded to get his own plate of chicken, ribs, baked beans, and corn on the cob. When their drinks were served, they dug in with gusto.

During the next hour, Paige told Alec about her day in Barbados and promised to show him around Bridgetown on the return trip. Alec told her about his evening with the Sheffields. As they were finishing their meal, Alec asked, "What do you think of them?"

Wiping the last of the barbeque sauce from her mouth, Paige replied, "I like Nora a lot. She was very sympathetic to me when a bee stung my wrist. Maggie just made me feel like I was wasting her time.

"As to Jeffrey, he seems a likable sort of fellow. He fixed my toilet a few weeks ago. I forgot the vacuum system was so sensitive and flushed down a make-up remover pad."

Alec grinned as he remembered Jeffrey's tall tales. "What's your opinion of Rick Tanner?"

Paige wrinkled her noise in disapproval, "I don't trust him at all. His office is adjacent to my desk. I've often seen female passengers disappear in there only to emerge several hours later quite disheveled."

"Since his engagement, has he been up to any shenanigans?"

"No. It's been quiet. Widi would know if he moved his extracurricular activities to his cabin. He cleans Rick's stateroom too."

Alec decided to see Widarta in the morning to ask about Rick's sexual pursuits and Scott's alibi. Curious about the cruise director's gambling habits, Alec asked, "Have you ever seen him in the casino?"

Paige was about to respond when she indicated to Alec that Rick was in line for the outdoor buffet. Beside him, laughing and looking very chummy, was Gwen. Paige lowered her voice fearful it would carry. "I don't go into the casino much. Those bells and whistles drive me crazy. I've heard, though, that Rick is fond of blackjack. Gwen told me one day at the pool."

With the information he'd amassed so far, Alec felt nearly ready to confront Rick Tanner.

Over coffee and ice cream, Paige and Alec made small talk and watched the serving staff clear away the buffet tables of food. Some of the children were already in the pool and the adults were making a beeline for the hot tubs. A band was beginning to set up for the evening's entertainment. Once again, Alec felt at peace with the world. He could almost hear Shanna telling him to live again. He caught Paige looking at him with a perplexed expression. This time it was Paige's turn to ask, "Are you okay?"

Smiling, Alec took her hand and kissed it tenderly. "I'm more than okay." Before long, they were dancing to old favorites, such as "Earth

Angel" and "Surfer Girl." Even though Alec wasn't an especially experienced dancer, he knew how to lead. Paige was able to follow his footsteps easily.

A little after ten, Rick took the microphone and announced that the sail-away fireworks were about to begin beside the salt-water pool on the Riviera Deck. Most of the passengers began to move in that direction. Alec and Paige wanted to spend some time alone, but they followed behind the crowd.

Alec was glad they didn't miss the dazzling display of lights. While Paige leaned against him, Alec kissed the back of her ears and neck. He tightened his grasp around her waist as she trembled against him. After the fireworks ended, Alec murmured, "Let's go find a place to do some serious necking."

Paige turned to face him. "Do you want to go back to my cabin?"

Alec wanted to with every fiber of his being, but replied, "Lass, once we make love, I won't be able to stop. I'll want to bed you every night and wake up with you each morning. Are you ready for that?"

Blushing, Paige whispered, "I'll be ready when you are."

Deciding to look for an out-of-the way spot on the ship, Paige suggested a secluded area below the Lower Promenade Deck. As they got closer to the hideaway, they heard the voices of a man and a woman who probably had the same idea. Alec and Paige were about to slip away when Alec stopped and whispered, "I think it's Rick and Gwen."

Not above eavesdropping, Alec led Paige into the shadows and listened.

Gwen declared, "Rick, I don't understand. You just said you love me. Why are you marrying her?"

"She has money," answered Rick, as though he were explaining to a child.

"Are you sure she's rich?"

"Yeah. Her ex is some kind of world-famous plastic surgeon from New York. When Janet thought he was having an affair with one of his patients, she hired a private dick to spy on him. He was caught in the act and forced to pay her a huge settlement."

"Why can't your father help you pay off your gambling debts?"

"Gwen, I told you. The old geezer refuses to give me any more money, and he *wants* me to marry Janet. He thinks she'll straighten me out. For a wedding present, he's shelling out some big bucks for our initiation dues to Greenwood Hunt Club in Boca. It's worth a small fortune!"

"But you don't even play golf or tennis."

Rick's voice suddenly became very harsh. "Don't you see? By marrying Janet, I'll not only get *her* money, I'll also win back *my* family's approval."

CHAPTER 8

▼

"I'LL MAKE LOVE TO YOU"

Words & Music—Kenneth Edmonds

Saturday Morning—28th of January

The next day, Alec hurried to his office to delve into the casino's income and expense reports. Having overheard Rick and Gwen's conversation, Alec hoped to find tangible proof of Rick's financial difficulties.

Alec discovered that most of the casino's income came from roulette, craps, blackjack, and Caribbean stud poker, as well as an inordinate number of slot machines. Passengers with money to burn could also purchase scratch cards, lotto tickets, seats in tournaments, and pay a 3% surcharge for drawing cash from their credit cards.

Although the reports specified how much each game took in, Alec couldn't tell how much the cruise director lost. He decided to fall back on his original plan and talk to the blackjack dealers when the ship left Martinique at two.

Just as Alec was wondering what to do next, he heard a soft knock at the door. Alec called, "Come in," and started to walk to the outer office. He welcomed Widi as he entered the room and said, "I see you got my message."

Widarta looked distressed and meekly asked, "Did I do something wrong?"

Not realizing how his note would appear, Alec immediately tried to put him at ease. "Oh no, you've been doing a splendid job. I wanted you to come here because I need your help."

Widarta relaxed and his perpetual smile returned. "What can I do?"

Alec wasn't sure how to pose his question. He first explained that he was helping the police investigate Mark Linley's death. After a slight pause, he continued. "Can you tell me what you saw on the morning of the controller's death, and who has been sleeping with who? I particularly need to know about Scott Harris, Gwen Llewelyn, Rick Tanner, and Mark Linley."

"That's easy!" exclaimed Widi. "My friend Isa can help too. He cleans the rooms at the other end of A Deck."

Eager now to obtain the information, Alec launched into his questions. "On the 22nd, did you see Eric Santos come out of Scott's cabin?"

Widi smiled as he recalled that morning. "He tried to sneak out without being seen. But I caught him. It was after 7:00."

"What time did Rick Tanner leave his stateroom?"

"I missed him, but I saw his friend, the dark-haired lady. She likes to go running on the Sun Deck every morning."

"When his girlfriend isn't onboard, does Gwen *sleep* with him?"

"She used to stay overnight. But not since Thanksgiving when he told everyone he was getting married."

"Did you happen to see Mark Linley before he left for the gym?"

Widi thought for a while. "The girl from the spa was with him a few times that week, but on the day he died, he was alone. I saw him about five that morning." Widarta hesitated a moment and then quickly added, "I wasn't there the whole time. For about an hour, I helped Isa fold sheets in the laundry."

Even though Alec didn't learn anything new, he was relieved to hear that his assumptions had been correct. He walked Widi to the office door and told him that he was grateful for his help. As he was leaving, Widarta turned to Alec and said timidly, "Miss Paige is a very pretty lady. No one ever visits her. I think you should."

A smile played upon Alec's lips as he replied, "I may just do that."

Before Alec and Paige had parted last night, they agreed to meet the following day for dinner and a movie. The planned to see an Alfred Hitchcock film that was being shown in the ship's cinema. Alec wasn't entirely sure how they were going to spend the rest of the evening. A big part of him wanted to follow Widi's advice.

Ready for a break, Alec decided to find Douglas and drag him to lunch. He last saw him on Thursday when they had drinks with the Sheffields.

Maggie and Nora were busy sorting through a stack of forms in the infirmary when Alec arrived on the scene. Despite Maggie's usual scowl, Nora greeted Alec enthusiastically and beckoned him over. "I have something for you."

She walked over to her handbag that was hanging on the back of a chair. From an inside pocket, she removed a folded piece of paper and handed it to Alec. "Jeffrey made you a copy of the plumbing log."

Alec tucked the list into his breast pocket, happy to have something to do that afternoon. After extending his thanks, he asked Nora, "Where is the old sawbones?"

Laughing, she replied. "He just went to lunch a few minutes ago. If you rush, you may be able to catch him!"

Alec said goodbye and hurried off. Moments later, he found Douglas at a table for two, munching on a grilled cheese sandwich.

Douglas indicated to Alec to take the vacant chair with a nod of his head.

Still standing, Alec remarked, "I'll be right back. That sandwich looks good."

When Alec returned, his plate was laden with more than a sandwich. He had French fries, a grilled Reuben, apple pie, and coffee. He quickly took a seat and began to eat.

Alec told him about his inquiries between bites. "Last night, Paige and I overheard a very interesting conversation between Rick and Gwen."

Douglas looked up from his plate and leered. "Now, what were they up to?"

"Not what you think," countered Alec. Rick told Gwen that he's marrying Janet Kane for her money. Apparently, Janet received a hefty settlement from her ex-husband, a plastic surgeon from New York."

"By God, I bet she was married to Charles Kane!"

"Who's he?" Alec demanded.

Warming to the subject, Douglas explained, "I read an article about Dr. Charles Kane in *Time* or *Newsweek*. If he's the one I'm thinking about, he pioneered a technique in surgery that drastically reduces the risk of scaring in keloid-prone patients. He's worth a small fortune and quite a womanizer."

Alec wondered why some women gravitated to men of that kind. He hoped that Janet would eventually see through Rick's scheme and asked Douglas whether she should be warned. The doctor, always cautious, thought it best not to interfere.

Moving to a more agreeable topic, Douglas asked, "How are you getting on with our future-cruise consultant?"

Alec sighed. "Paige has helped me feel like a man again. I don't know how much longer I'll be able to resist her."

"Why would you even try?" gasped Douglas.

"I lost Shanna only six months ago. It may be too soon for me to get involved with another woman."

Douglas's expression softened as he replied. "My dear boy, I was much older than you when my wife died. But I know that you've got to go on with your life. You're still a young man, and Shanna wouldn't want you to be alone."

Alec cast a grateful glance at Douglas, as he removed Jeffrey's list from his pocket. Alec scanned the repair log and realized that he'd need more information before setting out on his quest. He had no idea which cabin was assigned to whom.

His lunch long finished, Alec got up from the table and said to Douglas in his best Holmesian tone, "Murder's afoot." Though it wasn't quite true, it sounded far preferable to saying, "I'm about to visit every public lavatory on this plumbing log."

Armed with a passenger manifest from the proceeding cruise and an up-to-date record of crew cabins, Alec began to "stalk his porcelain prey." He learned that three public toilets were out of commission on the day of Mark Linley's death.

The plumbers could not determine a reason for a back up in the handicapped lavatory on the Lower Promenade Deck. The ladies' room toilet next to the children's activity center had been clogged with baby wipes, and the men's room in the gym was stuffed up by a tea bag. Alec couldn't fathom how a tea bag found its way into the system, but was generally disappointed with the findings.

From the passenger manifest, Alec was able to cross check Miss Kane's cabin number with those on Jeffrey's list. Janet's toilet worked fine that day.

Among the crew, Alec was most interested to discover that Gwen reported a blockage on the 22nd. According to the log, a book of casino matches was retrieved from her vacuum system. Having a suspicious nature, Alec speculated that Gwen found those matches at the scene of the crime and flushed them down the toilet, thinking they had belonged to Rick.

As Alec was planning his next move, the horns on the Pegasus blared, declaring its intention to sail. Since the ship would soon be returning to international waters, Alec walked over to Casino Bar and took a seat on one of the stools.

From his perch, Alec watched a few casino staff members go into the gaming area. When he saw a young man take his place behind a semi-circular table, Alec began to approach him. From seemingly nowhere, the pit boss emerged and warned, "I'm sorry sir. I can't let you in yet."

On Flagship Cruises, the casino was operated by an outside concession. Alec needed to be careful, literally and figuratively, about crossing the line. The casino still had to meet the monetary goals specified in its contract, but it was the responsibility of the pit boss to oversee the security needs of his staff.

Alec backed away from the area and apologized. "I'm sorry to disturb you, but I could use your help. My name is Alec DunBarton, and I'm serving as the Liaison Officer between this ship and the Fort Lauderdale Sheriff's Office. I'd like to have a word with your blackjack dealers about one of your patrons."

The pit boss responded belligerently. "I can't allow that. Information of that kind is strictly confidential and requires a court order."

Unsure whether it was true, Alec retorted with a cool, "I see." As Alec turned away, he tried to memorize the faces of the dealers in the room beyond. He would find another time to speak to them.

The rest of the day went from bad to worse. At 4:00 o'clock, Alec entered the Bull Dog Pub hoping to learn something that would connect Rick Tanner to the murder. In one of the bar's leathered upholstered booths, Alec ordered an afternoon pick-me-up and jotted down several questions.

On a paper napkin, Alec scribbled, "Where were you when Mark Linley died? How did you get along with the controller? Did he try to blackmail you over your DWI arrest or your gambling activities?" None of those questions would be asked.

Rick arrived late and sat down briefly. Before Alec could open his mouth, he said, "I decided it would be a waste of time for me to speak to you about the murder. As far as I'm concerned your title is meaningless, and the captain can't force me to tell you anything. If your buddy McGill wants to know something, he knows where to find me." With that said, Rick rose to his feet and sauntered out of the bar.

Alec mulled over Rick's words and concluded he was right. He had no real authority. So far, he had been able to uncover some financial discrepancies and elicit gossip from his coworkers. Alec realized that motive and opportunity weren't going to be enough to solve this crime. In order to catch Linley's killer and regain a sense of his own worthiness, he would need incontrovertible evidence.

Although Alec felt somewhat deflated after his run in with the casino manager and Rick Tanner, he didn't let it ruin his meal with Paige. As planned, he took her to the Rainbow Grill, a specialty restaurant onboard the ship. Passengers and crew alike were charged a "nominal" fee to dine in the reservations-only environment.

To Alec it was well worth the cost. The atmosphere was subdued and the food superb. They consumed huge pieces of shrimp and lobster in a delicate Newburg sauce. After finishing the first four courses, Alec discovered for once, there was no room for dessert.

They followed dinner with a movie. The only thing that disturbed Alec was his inability to "make out" with Paige in the darkened theatre. The armrest continually got in his way. Every time Alec moved in for a kiss, he banged his elbow and Paige chuckled. He couldn't remember having had this much trouble as a teenager.

By the time *Rear Window* ended, both of them were yawning and ready for bed. While Alec walked Paige to her cabin, he fell uncharacteristically silent. Paige seemed to notice he had something on his mind. At her door, she asked, "Do you want to come in and talk?"

Alec agreed and followed behind her. Almost immediately, he blurted out, "I want to make love to you!"

In answer to his declaration, Paige pressed her body close to his and whispered, "Tomorrow?"

Gently at first and then more intensely, Alec kissed her until they were both breathless. Not wanting to ruin his plans for their upcoming evening, Alec made a date to meet Paige for cocktails at seven in the Constellation Lounge. He gave her one more kiss and left.

When Alec entered his stateroom, he realized that he was singing the song, "I'll Make Love to You." As he recalled *all* the lyrics, Alec nearly blushed. The words, "for tonight is just your night, we're gonna celebrate, all thru the night," expressed everything that was on his mind. Though Alec wanted to get some rest, sleep eluded him for hours.

The next morning, Alec was in no mood to go to his office or to look around for Mark's murderer. Frankly, he was running out of ideas and decided to prepare for his date with Paige instead.

During the next few hours, Alec rearranged his cabin and made several purchases at the shopping arcade. By noon, his cabin was well stocked with all the essentials. A waiter in the dining room lent Alec two wine glasses and a standing champagne bucket. Widi, his fairy godfather, was especially helpful. He rustled up candles and made Alec's twin beds into an inviting king. When he was finished, Alec's room resembled a honeymoon suite in a five-star hotel.

With his night set, Alec checked his e-mail, hoping that a message from McGill would revive his flagging investigation. Alec was not disappointed. He double clicked his in box and read its contents.

Subj: Continuing Investigation of Linley Homicide
Date: 28th January, 10:15:07 PM EST
From: Dan.McGill@coflso.net
To: AlecDunBarton@aol.com

I'm glad you're making progress. Our inquiries have been moving along slowly and I feel frustrated that I'm unable to carry out a normal investigation. You've been invaluabie to my department and me.

When the Pegasus returns to port on Wednesday, I want to see Gwen Llewelyn, Scott Harris, Paige Anderson, Michelle Van Dam, and Rick Tanner. It's come to my attention that Tanner owes a bundle to some tough customers in Miami.

I've been able to review a portion of the HR files. On your end, I want you to interview Ronald Bauer. On two separate occasions, he sent letters of complaint to the cruise line asking them to fire Mark Linley. Bauer didn't mention names, but wrote that a nurse (probably Sheffield) and the shore excursion manager were "victims of his cruel attacks." Please confirm their identities and question them.

I also have one promising lead. I checked Linley's former employment record with the Internal Revenue and learned that several people complained about his audit techniques. In cross-referencing them with the passenger manifest, I found a couple from Chicago. I'll let keep you posted.

Dan McGill

Even though Alec knew that McGill would want to interview Paige, he was, nonetheless, upset to see her name in print. Alec knew he was allow-ing his personal feelings toward her convince him that she had nothing to do with Linley's death. He hoped for the second time that his intuition wasn't leading him astray.

Alec was pleased to hear about Rick's predicament. At the moment, he could think of nothing more gratifying than watching a mobster break the cruise director's legs. With regret, Alec tabled that thought and left the Dolphin Lounge to find Ronald Bauer. Once again, the case looked promising.

When Alec returned to his cabin to get ready for the evening, he felt a mixture of elation and dread. He was thrilled with the information from Bauer and anxious about his upcoming date with Paige.

Alec turned off the water just in time to hear Widarta shout, "Please, open the door, Mr. Alec. I have your uniform."

Before letting him in, Alec wiped off shaving cream from his neck and ears, and threw on his robe.

With gratitude, he took the hanger from Widi and muttered, "I don't know what I'd do without you. I forgot it was the second formal night on the Pegasus."

Widi grinned. "I think you have other things on your mind!"

"You're right. I have a bad case of the jitters."

"Jitters?"

"Oh you know, I'm a bit nervous."

Widarta shyly patted Alec on the back. "Don't worry. Miss Paige really likes you. I'll be back later to chill your champagne and make the room nice." As the cabin steward left, Alec heard him say, "Widi will take care of everything."

All of a sudden, Alec burst out laughing. He felt like a forty-two year old "virgin" on his first date. He had no time for this nonsense. He still needed to dress and pick up some dinner.

At seven, Alec met Paige at the entrance to the Constellation Lounge. She was enticingly dressed in a long, black strapless gown. Her tan shoulders were bare and a slit at the side of her dress climbed to her mid thigh. Alec's first instinct was to slip his hands along her shapely legs.

Paige peered into the crowded room, and said coyly, "It's pretty crowded in there. Would you like to go somewhere quieter?"

Alec's eyes sparkled in response. "It's funny you should say that. I know a place on A Deck that has candlelight and champagne. How does that sound?"

Paige took his arm and sighed, "It sounds wonderful."

They made their way down to Alec's cabin, chatting happily. At the door, Alec fumbled with his plastic key card. Noting his awkwardness, Paige said, "Come here. I think a kiss may steady your hand."

Paige grazed her lips against his until Alec responded with fervor. With his arms still wrapped around her, he swiped the key in the lock and pulled her inside.

The room looked magical. A music station on the television was playing "old standards." The candlelight appeared to be swaying to the song "Night and Day" by Cole Porter.

On seeing the cabin, Paige exclaimed, "Oh Alec, this is incredible. When did you find time to do this?"

"I did the scavenging, but our friend Widi helped me decorate. Do you like it?"

In a husky voice, she replied, "I like you."

Alec pulled her close and they began to dance to the song. Paige took a moment to slip off her heels and then settled back into his arms. As they continued to move to the music Alec buried his face in her hair and whispered, "Lass, you don't know what you do to me."

Paige replied with kisses that begged for a response. When Alec answered with his entire being, she hoarsely pleaded, "Make love to me."

Together, they edged closer to the bed. Again Alec felt clumsy and Paige seemed to read his mind. She helped Alec remove his coat and bowtie.

After she undid his shirt buttons, she turned around and asked Alec to unzip her dress. When it fell in a heap on the floor, Paige faced him, revealing her body. Unable to stand the tension any longer, Alec deposited Paige on the bed.

For a while, Alec was satisfied kissing her mouth and neck. As his yearning for her grew, he began to explore her body with an overriding passion that was born out of hunger and loneliness.

CHAPTER 9

▼

"A VIEW TO A KILL"

Words & Music—John Barry, Nicholas Bates, Simon Le Bon,
Andrew Taylor, John Taylor, and Roger Taylor

Monday Morning—30ᵗʰ of January

Alec woke up feeling mischievous and began to nibble on Paige's earlobe.
She shivered as his stubbly beard grazed her neck and shoulder. Smiling,
Paige turned to face him and asked, "What time is it?"

Alec twisted around and glanced at the alarm clock on the end table.
"It's almost eight thirty."

Paige let out a shriek and scrambled out of bed naked. Slipping on
Alec's tee shirt that was beside the bed, she protested, "Why didn't you
wake me sooner? I'm going to be late."

Alec couldn't take his eyes off her. With supreme effort he focused his
attention on her question and replied. "Lass, we didn't get to sleep until
early this morning. You needed a little lie in."

Paige gathered up her dress, shoes, and key. She bent over Alec and gave
him a kiss that promised many more rousing nights. Scampering out the
door, she called, "I'll see *you* later."

Alec grinned. His shirt barely covered her luscious bottom. It was a
good thing that her stateroom was only thirty feet down the hall.

Feeling fully content with life, Alec got out of bed and started to tidy the cabin. As he rinsed out glasses and gathered up trash, he smiled reviewing how they spent the night together.

Alec's first stop after breakfast was the infirmary. In order to pursue the detective's line of inquiry, Alec needed to touch base with Nora Sheffield. She *was* the nurse who Bauer had referred to in his letter to headquarters.

Luck was with him. When Alec entered the waiting room, no sick passengers were demanding attention, and both Nora and Jeffrey were present. After exchanging a few pleasantries, Alec got right to the point and said, "McGill wanted to know how the security chief learned of your quarrel with Mark Linley."

Nora looked to her husband for help with the details. Before she could reply, Jeffrey intervened. "When that fool insulted Nora over those tongue depressors, it pissed me off no end. I told Nora he should be taught a lesson, but she didn't want me to make matters worse. In the end, we compromised and told Bauer."

Nora nodded in agreement. "Jeffrey spoke to him the following day."

"What was Bauer's response?" queried Alec.

Jeffrey smirked as he recalled the incident. "You know, he became angry and his ears turned bright pink. Up until then, I thought Bauer was pretty mild mannered. After he calmed down, he said we should leave it up to him. I got the feeling he tangled with him in the past over something personal."

Alec hadn't considered that likelihood, but it was certainly feasible. Earlier, the chief of security told Alec he'd also written a letter of complaint on behalf of the shore excursion assistant manager, Milos Radovanovic. Alec expected that a chat with Milos would shed some light on Jeffrey's theory. Impatient to question Milos next, Alec left, but not before asking Douglas to meet him and Paige for dinner that evening.

Alec arrived at the excursion office just as it opened. There was already a long line for tickets. The last stop on the ship's itinerary was the cruise line's private island, Coral Cay, in the Bahamas. Even though many of the activities on the island were free, passengers were more than willing to wait in line and pay extra fees to rent catamarans, snorkel gear, kayaks, and sun-fish sailboats. For the less adventurous, there was also an historic nature walk and a glass-bottom boat ride.

After Alec learned that Milos would be occupied till noon when the tour desk closed, the two men agreed to meet for lunch. With almost two hours to kill, Alec headed to his office. He hadn't yet audited the shore excursion receipts. Perhaps Mark Linley had reason to suspect Milos Radovanovic of wrongdoing.

On the way to the Lido Deck, Alec and Milos discussed some of the attractions on Coral Cay. Milos mentioned there would be live music and an outdoor barbeque luncheon on the island. Passengers could also have their hair braided at the West Indian marketplace and take part in Gwen's dancercise class on the beach. After hearing about the activities, Alec promptly decided to go ashore. It would give him an opportunity to try out his land legs and tell Gwen that McGill wanted to see her on Wednesday.

Alec soon found himself enjoying the young man's company. Milos was easygoing and had a dry sense of humor. As they were lunching, Alec brought up the murder investigation and asked him about his argument with Mark.

"It was over a ridiculous thing," Milos replied. "While the controller was going over the shore excursion confirmation tickets, he complained that some of the dates were marked incorrectly. Usually when he got into a snit, I merely yessed him to death. That day, there was no pleasing him, and he called me an idiot in front of several passengers."

Milos took a gulp of lemonade and shook his head indifferently. "I didn't care and was ready to let the whole thing drop. Somehow the chief of security heard about the incident and asked me if *he* could report it. I agreed. It seemed important to him."

Alec found Milos Radovanovic's response significant. Curious about the timing, Alec queried, "When did Bauer question you about Linley's behavior?"

"About two days after it happened."

"And when did all this occur?"

"Oh. Not more than three weeks ago. What do you think Officer Bauer really wanted?"

Alec didn't know, and he left that question unanswered. During the rest of their meal, Milos told Alec about growing up in Serbia. Even though Alec enjoyed talking to him, his thoughts were elsewhere, and he soon thanked Milos and departed.

Since the accounts of the excursion desk had been squeaky clean, Alec was anxious to return to his office once again and check the expenditures of Security Officer Bauer and those of his department. Maybe this time he would uncover something more vital to the case.

At six o'clock on the dot, Paige opened the door in answer to Alec's knock. She looked alluring in her plain white uniform and Alec, without delay, moved in for an embrace and long kiss. Paige, not too subtlety, needed to remind him that they had a dinner date with Dr. Abbot.

Douglas was standing in front of the restaurant when they arrived.

While they glanced around the room for a place to sit, Alec suggested, "Why don't we take a table outside by the pool."

Paige turned to Douglas and said, "I think he has an ulterior motive. It's the only place on board where he can smoke his pipe."

The doctor laughed and replied, "Alec, I believe she has your number,"

Spying a vacant table near the Lido Bar, Paige went to save it as Alec and Douglas headed for the buffet. That night, British fare was being offered.

When they joined the back of the line, Douglas remarked, "You look smitten."

Alec's face beamed at the same time that the doctor's features clouded over with anxiety.

Stumbling over his words, Douglas asked, "You…'re, you're certain, aren't you, that Paige had nothing to do with Linley's death?"

Alec was startled by his question. Not sure whether to be angry with his good friend or amused, he responded, "Why are you asking? Did you *hear* something?"

Douglas instantly tried to relieve Alec's fears. "I haven't heard a thing. I'm just concerned about you. After grieving over Shanna and Emma, it would be horrible to lose someone else." Placing a hand on Alec's shoulder, he added, "Don't let an old man's worries spoil your evening."

Alec didn't need to hear Douglas's words to be prepared for the worst. Since that awful day in August, Alec had been waiting for the other shoe to drop. He knew that life was capricious and could change in a blink of an eye.

The doctor's expression remained troubled as Alec interjected, "Look, I can't explain it logically. But, my sixth sense tells me that Paige had nothing to do with Mark Linley's murder. I'm sure it will be proven right."

Feeling more optimistic, he and Douglas returned to the table with dishes of steak and kidney pie, fish and chips, and Shepherd's pie. Paige gaped at the mountains of food and exclaimed, "What? No haggis?"

Alec gave Paige a tolerant smile. "Now Lass, if you expect a wee kiss or two tonight, you'd better not mock my food." Acting like a naughty child, Paige responded by simply sticking out her tongue.

After a hearty meal, the trio moved a few seats over to the Lido Bar for drinks. They weren't sitting out long before Alec spotted Gwen and Boyd coming toward them from the direction of the spa. Douglas invited them to take a seat and gave the waiter their beverage orders.

Once everyone was served, Boyd stood up and announced that a well-known talent agent had been watching him perform at various venues throughout the ship and offered him a job. Gwen gleefully chirped in, "They want him to be a studio musician in New York City! The gig would pay way more than he gets here. And he may even get a chance to tour with a really famous group. Isn't that great?"

Boyd looked at Gwen adoringly. For Alec, it was the first time he saw the fitness director without *any* artifice or pretense. He hoped to see a lot more of this side of Gwen.

Noticing Boyd still standing, Douglas asked, "You seem to have something else on your mind. Speak up and tell us what it is."

"Well," he began, "My contract with Flagship Cruise Line ends in a few weeks and Gwen's a month later." Looking at her shyly, he continued. "I sort of hoped she'd want to marry me then and move to the Big Apple."

As Boyd spoke those words, Gwen leaped from her chair and jumped into his waiting arms. While Paige and Douglas smiled at the exuberance of young love, Alec cynically wondered how Rick Tanner would take the news.

Shortly after Boyd proposed, the couple left hand in hand. Realizing he forgot to tell Gwen about McGill's summons, Alec said out loud, "It will be fun to visit her on the beach tomorrow."

On hearing he was going ashore, Douglas asked Alec, "Can you help me transport equipment from the tender to the medical facility on the island?"

Alec replied in an amazed tone, "What? We have to take a boat?"

"Unless you want to get your feet very wet!" laughed Douglas.

Paige smiled at their antics and explained. "The Pegasus is too large to dock at the coral reef marina. We *all* have to take a ten-minute tender ride to get to Coral Cay."

Douglas added, "It's one of the reasons we needed to set up a second infirmary." For the next few minutes the doctor told Paige and Alec about some of the predicaments his harebrained patients encountered on the secluded isle.

It was about ten when the trio finally broke up. Alec could see that Paige was exhausted, and he was definitely ready for bed. While he helped her to her feet, Paige said, "I'm not sure if it's the damp night air or watching those lovebirds, but I feel pretty old."

Alec grinned as they tottered off to his cabin.

The next morning, Alec woke up to find a steaming mug of coffee on his end table and Paige standing at his bedside. Before rushing off, she gave him a kiss on the forehead. From the cabin door she called, "Don't forget to come by the Welcome Center. I'll be there from eight to twelve."

Alec glanced at the clock and realized that he couldn't dally either. He had just twenty minutes to finish his coffee, shower, dress, and meet Douglas at the cargo-loading bay.

On his arrival, Alec apologized for being late and helped Douglas carry several heavy boxes onto the Pegasus lifeboat, which was serving as a tender. As they took their seats, Alec found himself looking forward to visiting the island paradise.

Later that morning, Alec discovered an ideal place on the bluff to watch Gwen conduct her dancercise class. She concluded the session with the theme song from the Bond film, *A View to a Kill*. While Alec sang along with Duran Duran, he experienced a sense of foreboding. The lyrics— "Dance into the fire, that fatal kiss is all we need. Dance into the fire, to fatal sounds of broken dreams"—simply gave him the chills.

After the class dispersed, Gwen turned off her boom box and got ready to sunbathe in the warm sun. She removed her leotard to expose a black and white string bikini. Once she adjusted her straps and arranged herself on several beach towels, she slathered on suntan oil. After taking a drink from her water bottle, Gwen lay down.

Deciding that it was a perfect time to speak to her, Alec trudged through the billowy white sand and took a seat on the corner of her towel. "Congrats again on your engagement," he exclaimed. "Did you celebrate last night?"

Gwen smiled dreamily. "It was wonderful. Boyd and I stopped at the jewelry boutique after we left you." Placing her hand on Alec's arms, she gushed, "Look what he bought me!"

Alec glanced down at the engagement ring. It was a brilliant, simply set, round diamond that almost matched the sparkle in Gwen's eyes.

"I did…n't want him to spend too much on it. But he said I was worth ev…ery penny."

"It's a beauty Gwen."

"Even…though we both don't drink, we al…so had a little champ…agne. Later, we we…nt for a…wa…lk on…t…pr…"

Gwen's speech became increasingly incoherent and her breathing sporadic.

Not sure whether she was choking, Alec pulled her up to an upright position and started to pat her back. Growing concerned, Alec said, "Are you okay?"

Gwen looked directly at Alec with no recognition. Her eyes lolled back toward her head, exposing just the whites. Though her skin was covered with suntan lotion, Alec noticed beads of perspiration mixing in with the oily substance. Something was terribly wrong.

Without any further hesitation, Alec picked her up and carried her to the island infirmary. At the front door, Alec yelled for the doctor. "Quick. Please, come quickly! For God's sake, where are you?"

Alec placed Gwen gently down on an examining table in a small room off the waiting area. Douglas came in complaining about the commotion, but stopped when he saw Gwen. The doctor shouted for Beth to come straight away, and she was at his side within seconds. As they worked together to resuscitate her, Alec stood by the door feeling utterly helpless.

Alec wasn't sure how much time passed. It seemed surreal. As he waited, he tried to figure out what caused Gwen to fall ill. Did she experience heat exhaustion or have an allergic reaction to an insect bite? Did the champagne affect her system in an odd way? Lastly, he thought, "She must pull through. Her life has just begun to turn around."

Suddenly, the room took on an eerie silence. Douglas looked at the clock on the wall. "It's no good, Beth. She's gone. Time of death, 11:04 A.M."

Beth began to cry and her tears mirrored Alec's inner turmoil. A voice inside Alec's head screamed, "How could she be dead? Just moments ago, she was dancing."

CHAPTER 10

▼

"NEW YORK MINUTE"

Words & Music—Don Henley/Danny Kortchmar/Jai Winding

Tuesday Morning—31ˢᵗ of January

Alec left the island infirmary intending to contact Jarvis and Bauer right away. Gwen was dead and there was no time to waste.

While he stumbled along the dirt path, Alec tried to remember what Douglas told him to do. He felt so worn out and hot. Unable to catch his breath or focus his thoughts, Alec wandered into the Welcome Center. The building was cool and dark. He needed to sit down and sort it out.

Paige dashed to Alec's side as he staggered into the room. Her expression of concern intensified when she noticed his appearance. His uniform was covered with fine grains of sand and grease stains. Alec's face was drenched with perspiration and his hair was in disarray. Paige guided him to a nearby chair and reached for a bottle of water that was chilling in an ice chest by the door. While she twisted off the cap, she asked, "Alec, are you all right?"

Alec gazed at her as if he were seeing her for the first time. "I'm feeling a bit dizzy, that's all."

Paige didn't seem satisfied with his explanation. She gave him the water and said, "Drink some. You may be dehydrated."

He extended his hand toward it, but had trouble seizing the bottle. Alec took a small sip, grimaced, and gave it back. "I'm too nauseous to drink it."

Resolutely, Paige called her coworker. "Maurice, can you help me? I think Mr. DunBarton needs to go to the infirmary."

A young man came out from behind the counter and assisted Alec to his feet. Even though Alec protested that he could walk on his own, he tripped a few times on the way to the medical hut. Paige and Maurice got him there just as he retched into a pail by the front door.

While Maurice helped Alec to a seat in the waiting area, Douglas rushed to the examining room to grab his stethoscope and blood pressure cuff. When he returned, the doctor immediately began to check Alec's vital signs and hoarsely inquired, "Do you know what happened?"

Paige's voice throbbed with emotion as she replied. "He came into the center looking weak and disoriented. Moments ago he vomited, and I think he's also having trouble breathing."

Once the doctor finished examining him, he looked up and gave Paige a reassuring smile. "Alec appears to be okay now. His heart rate is a bit rapid, but within normal range, and there's no evidence of respiratory distress."

Paige heaved a sigh of relief and told Maurice that he could return to work. Before he left, Douglas added, "When you get back to the Welcome Center, can you please radio Captain Jarvis and Officer Bauer, and let them know they're needed at the island infirmary?"

Douglas monitored Alec's other functions as Paige observed. Alec allowed the doctor to poke and prod him for a little while. When the doctor shined a penlight into his eyes, he snapped, "Stop fussing, will you? I'm feeling better."

Getting to the heart of the matter, the doctor asked, "Do you think your symptoms were like those of Gwen's?"

Clearly bewildered, Paige cut in. "What's going on? Why did you tell Maurice to contact the captain, and what happened to Gwen?"

Alec answered Paige first and said, "Lass, I brought her to the infirmary about forty minutes ago. She died shortly later."

Addressing himself to Douglas, he continued. "I think our reactions were similar. When I spoke to her on the beach, she couldn't catch her breath, and she was drenched in perspiration."

Paige remained calm, but gasped when she saw that the table in the examining room was covered with a sheet. Pointing in that direction, she said, "Is she under there?"

Douglas got up to close the partially open door and confirmed Alec's statement. "Her physical state deteriorated rapidly. There was nothing I could do. Thank goodness, Alec's condition was less acute."

While Douglas spoke to Paige, Alec tried to comprehend the full meaning of the doctor's declaration. There was no longer any reason to believe that Gwen died from a heart attack or anaphylactic shock. Those ailments weren't contagious.

Speaking to no one in particular, Alec muttered, "Gwen's exercise class went without a hitch. She got ready to sunbathe, applied suntan oil, and gulped down some bottled water."

"Did the *water* make her sick?"

Paige's question caught Alec off guard and brought him out of his reverie. Suddenly, he made a move to stand up.

"Where do you think you're going?" barked Douglas, as he gently pushed Alec back into his chair.

"I've got to go! Gwen's things are on the beach. Don't you see? She was poisoned," shouted Alec. "I never touched Gwen's water. And I felt sick long before Paige gave me a drink in the Welcome Center. Her *suntan oil* must have been tainted."

Staring at the grains of sand still sticking to his arms, he added, "The oil rubbed against me when I carried her here. We can't leave that bottle on the beach. Someone may walk away with it."

Douglas was aware of the seriousness, but wouldn't let Alec get up until he felt stronger. Paige instantly volunteered to go, promising to use the doctor's latex gloves to transfer Gwen's belongings to a large trash bag. She knew where the class was held and assured Alec she'd be right back. Before Paige scurried off, Alec demanded a kiss. He was beginning to act more like himself.

Not taking any chances with Alec's health, Douglas cleaned off the sun-tan oil residue from his forearms with water, remarking that soap often increased the absorption rate of some topical poisons. While Alec was digesting that information, Bauer walked in.

Since Alec was the doctor's only patient, the chief of security spoke without his usual restraint, "Maurice contacted me at the Lifeguard Station. What did you want?"

Douglas told him what had occurred, along with Alec's involvement and subsequent illness. When the doctor finished, Bauer asked neutrally, "Do you think it was foul play?"

Eager to add his two cents, Alec interjected. "It could have been accidental. But to be honest, I think Gwen was poisoned by Mark Linley's killer."

In response, Bauer shook his head and mumbled, "Oh Gott. Nicht ein anderes." Although Alec didn't know any German, he surmised that the security chief was shaken by the news. Recovering himself, Bauer asked the doctor, "How do you want to handle this?"

Douglas pointed out that Gwen needed to be moved from the infirmary to the Pegasus's morgue and cooler as soon as possible. He didn't want to maneuver her body once rigor mortis set in. Bauer, on the other hand, wanted to protect the reputation of the cruise line and bring her back without being seen. Their solution was to convey her to the ship in a laundry cart covered with beach towels. Alec felt it was a shabby way to treat her, but couldn't think of a better plan.

Shortly after the security officer departed for the island laundry facilities, Paige returned with Gwen's compact disc player, water bottle, clothing, terry-cloth towels, tote bag, and suntan oil. Alec was relieved to see that she found everything.

Anxious to inform McGill of Gwen Llewelyn's death, Alec asked to be released. Douglas took Alec's vital signs again and gave him permission to take a few steps. Paige stood near him like a mother hen watching her baby chick.

Douglas cautioned, "You're to call me if any of your symptoms return. Beth will be returning with Maggie shortly. After they relieve me, I'll be in the morgue."

Paige and Alec left together carrying Gwen's belongings. After a brief stop at the Welcome Center to see Maurice, they were on their way. As the tender pulled away from the dock, Alec thought, "Island paradises aren't what they're cracked up to be."

Once back on the ship, Alec decided to speak to the captain first. Maurice hadn't been able to locate him prior to their leaving Coral Cay. When Alec and Paige parted at the loading bay, she whispered, "Please take care of yourself."

Although those words were lyrics to a song, Alec thought of "New York Minute" in which the Eagles sang, "In a New York Minute everything can change." It was so true that, "One day they're here; Next day they're gone." Deep in thought, Alec walked to the front desk. Gwen's death was starting to bring back some of the grief and vulnerability he felt when Shanna and Emma were first wrenched from him.

While Alec stowed away Gwen's personal effects in his office, a front-desk staff worker paged the captain. Alec reemerged from his office just as the captain approached. On seeing the liaison officer, Jarvis remarked dryly, "You wanted me?"

Alec ushered him into his office before responding. With the door safely closed behind them, he told the captain that Gwen was dead and probably murdered. Jarvis sat down at Scott's desk and shook his head in disbelief. Alec explained that the doctor and Bauer were in the process of transporting her corpse to the ship's morgue in a laundry cart. It took the captain some time to absorb the information.

Finally, he replied, "I don't see any reason to inform the Bahamian officials, since the island is privately owned by the cruise line. I want you to contact the Fort Lauderdale Sheriff's Department at once. Use the phone here, and bill it to the corporate cost center. In the meantime, I need to advise headquarters. I'll check back with you later. And for heaven's sake, please change. You look a disgrace!"

After the door shut, Alec looked down at his uniform and dusted off a few flecks of sand. As they dropped to the floor, he began to chuckle. It wasn't long before Alec's chuckle broke into a hearty laugh. He realized at that instant, his reaction was macabre. But it seemed to be the only way to deal with the shock.

Ready to make the call, Alec removed a writing pad from his desk drawer along with McGill's business card. He hoped the detective wasn't at lunch. It was just twelve thirty. Seconds later, the detective answered, "McGill here."

After clearing his throat, Alec said, "This is Alec DunBarton calling from the Pegasus. I'm afraid there's been another murder."

At the beginning of the conversation, Alec spoke steadily and described Gwen's illness and death. Later on, he frantically took notes and replied to McGill's questions in monosyllables. When he hung up the phone, Alec glanced at his list of instructions and hurried out of the office.

Alec's first stop was the ship's boutique. Aware of his messy appearance, Alec beckoned the sales person to the corner of the shop. Keeping his voice low, Alec enjoined, "I want you to remove all the Cruisin' Coconut suntan oil from your shelves until further notice."

"It's one of our best sellers. I'll have to get permission from my manager."

Alec wasn't in the mood for red tape. Succinctly, he stated, "The sheriff's office in Fort Lauderdale received a safety warning on this product. There's a possibility that it contains shards of glass. If your manager has any questions, he or she can contact me at extension 946."

On short notice, it was the best excuse Alec could come up with. He didn't want to alarm the shop's staff unduly. McGill thought it unlikely that the lotion was tampered with at the manufacturing or retail level, but he was obligated to take certain precautions.

Before leaving the shopping arcade, Alec picked up a bottle of Scotch from the duty-free store. Since his brush with death, Alec had been fighting bouts of nausea and a sense of apprehension. To him, whisky seemed the best solution.

Alec was in his stateroom toweling off from a hot shower and sipping Glenlivet when he heard a knock at the door. As he put on his robe, he called, "I'll be there in a minute."

His face fell when he saw it was Boyd. Alec knew that he had to be told, but he felt terribly unprepared to speak to him then and there.

Boyd looked puzzled as he entered. "Where's Gwen? I've been looking all over the place for her. Nurse Romano finally told me to see you. Is she hurt?"

Alec asked Boyd to sit down and poured him a large measure of Scotch. As he handed the glass to him, he said, "Laddy, I think you should take this."

Boyd waved it away. "I don't drink. Just tell me what happened to her."

Alec took the chair beside him and said in a hushed voice, "I'm sorry. Gwen had some sort of respiratory failure on the beach this morning. Although Dr. Abbot and Beth treated her within minutes, she couldn't be revived."

"She's dead?" he cried!

Alec nodded sadly. He knew from his own experience that there was nothing he could say or do to make it any easier for the young man. He handed him the drink once again and watched him gulp it down.

After a minute or two, Boyd composed himself and said, "Does the doctor know what made her si...ck?"

At this point, Alec wasn't sure how much to reveal. He thought it was probable that Gwen was poisoned, but he had no proof. There was also a chance that her suntan oil had been accidentally contaminated, or both he and Gwen had reacted to something entirely different. In any case, he knew it was no time to discuss their likelihoods.

Choosing his words carefully, Alec replied. "The doctor isn't certain yet. When we get into Fort Lauderdale tomorrow, her body will be sent to the medical examiner for an autopsy."

Boyd held out his glass for a refill and seemed satisfied for the moment. During the next half hour, Alec watched him go through a roller coaster of emotions from shock to anger and back to shock. When Boyd was ready to leave, Alec checked the interview schedule that McGill gave him over the telephone. Although he was reluctant to distress Boyd any further, Alec told him to come to the Dolphin Room at 2:15 tomorrow. Boyd shrugged his shoulders in resignation as he walked out the door.

Frustrated with the whole affair, Alec tossed back his drink, donned a clean uniform, and stepped into the corridor to search for Isa, Gwen's cabin steward. He found him in the Dolphin Room brewing coffee.

Per McGill's orders, Alec asked him about Gwen's habits and her late-night visitors. Like Widi, Isa was full of useful information. He told Alec that Gwen was with Boyd yesterday and they were very "lovey." When asked about her other male guests, he replied, "She was with Mr. Rick on Friday night. They went into her cabin and later on, I heard *arguing*. Is that the right word?"

"You mean they had a fight?"

"Yes, you know, she yelled at him and called him a name. Then, I heard the door slam. He was very mad and almost knocked me down in the hall."

"Do you know what happened after he left?"

Isa shook his head and merely said, "No."

At that point, Alec told Isa that Gwen was sick and would be in the infirmary overnight. Since McGill wanted Gwen's cabin secured until the crime scene unit arrived, Alec asked Isa to make sure that no one, including Bauer and Jarvis, gained admittance to her room. The cabin steward seemed to understand the serious nature of the situation and gravely promised he would. McGill wanted Alec to keep Gwen's death quiet until he had a word with the "suspects." For the rest of the afternoon, Alec notified those individuals at what time their interviews were scheduled.

At five o'clock, Alec returned to his cabin hoping to rest before dinner. Unfortunately, his telephone light was blinking with a message from the doctor telling him to come to Bauer's office at once. Alec took a few seconds to wash his face and went out to meet them.

Douglas answered Alec's knock almost instantly and admitted him. When he entered the room, Captain Jarvis acknowledged his presence and invited him to take a seat, remarking that they hadn't gotten to the "incident" yet.

Alec found himself getting annoyed by the captain's choice of words. Up until now, it seemed as though Gwen's death was being treated like a nuisance.

Straight away, Jarvis asked, "What did you learn from the homicide detective?"

Still irritated, Alec responded coolly. "McGill doesn't want Gwen's death to get out until he has the chance to speak with several people tomorrow. Earlier today, I had to tell her fiancé, Boyd Griffin, that Gwen died as a result of respiratory distress. If others ask about her condition, the detective feels we should merely say she's in the infirmary."

Alec glanced around the room to accentuate his point. "He plans to come aboard the Pegasus at 8:00 A.M." Gazing directly at Jarvis, he continued, "Is that agreeable with you?"

The captain replied, "That's fine." A moment later, he inquired, "Does he think Gwen's Llewelyn's death is related to Linley's and that she was murdered?"

Alec was less than honest at this point. Although, the answer to both questions was a resounding "yes," McGill didn't want *anyone* to know his game plan. He hoped to lull Gwen's killer into a false sense of security. Instead, Alec retorted, "McGill believes they may be separate, and Gwen might have been accidentally poisoned. He's especially eager to have her cabin inspected by the forensics unit."

Douglas spoke next, and he reported that Gwen's body had been wrapped in plastic and prepared for the medical examiner. When Bauer stated that no passengers got wind of her death, Jarvis replied, "Satisfactory," and stood up to leave.

As he was heading out the door, the captain stopped and turned to Alec. "By the way, the publicity and legal departments in London have agreed to drop criminal charges against Scott Harris in exchange for reparations. You'd better let McGill know that he'll be going ashore tomorrow. Headquarters also wants you to carry on as Liaison Officer."

"They bloody well better," thought Alec as he watched the captain depart.

Anxious to relax, Alec said good-bye to the others and made a beeline for Paige's cabin.

In answer to his knock, Paige flung open the door saying, "Where have you been? I've been so worried about you."

Alec took her in his arms and held her for quite a while, murmuring, "God, I've missed you!"

Paige looked at his tired face and said, "I'm gonna fetch some dinner from the officer's mess. We can have supper in your cabin and watch TV."

"That would be grand, Lass. You don't mind babysitting an old man?" Paige laughed at Alec's comment even though she was five years older than he.

An hour later, Alec was feeling considerably better. During dinner, he told Paige how Boyd took the grim news. From his voice, Paige seemed to realize how difficult the task had been for him. When Alec added that McGill wanted to see her in the morning, she made little of it.

Since Alec wasn't expecting any company that evening, he was startled by a loud knock at his door. Warily, Alec peered into the corridor and was relieved to see Gwen's cabin steward.

Speaking rapidly, Isa declared, "Mr. Rick came by. He wanted to get into Gwen's cabin and I told him *no*. He called me a fool and left."

Alec smiled wickedly and chortled, "Oh did he?"

Knowing that McGill would want to talk to Isa, Alec asked him to drop by the Dolphin Room at 8:30 A.M. Before he withdrew, Alec thanked him for his diligence.

After Alec and Paige cleared away the remnants of their dinner, they moved over to the bed to watch TV. While Alec surfed the channels, Paige propped up the pillows.

One of the stations was about to show *Die Another Day*. When Alec asked her whether she wanted to catch the movie, she readily agreed and said that she hadn't seen Pierce Brosnan star in any of the Bond films.

Amazed, Alec exclaimed, "So, you don't know that I look like him!"

Paige smiled in amusement. "Actually, the girls at the front desk told me that you two could be twins. I'd like to see for myself."

For the first fifteen minutes of the show, Alec watched her instead of the movie. Unable to stand the suspense any longer, he demanded, "Well, what do you think?"

Paige gave him a kiss and whispered. "I think *he* looks like *you*! But, he's too thin, and you're much more handsome." Alec was delighted with her response and sank down into the bedding. It wasn't long before he was fast asleep. A bit later, Paige began to doze, listening to James Bond, but lying next to the real McCoy.

CHAPTER 11

▼

"ANOTHER ONE BITES THE DUST"

Words & Music—John Deacon

Wednesday Morning—1st of February

"No, no. Stop it!" screamed Alec.

When he opened his eyes, Paige was peering at him with a troubled expression. "Are you all right? You were having a terrible dream. I didn't know whether or not to wake you."

Realizing that it was a nightmare, Alec smiled halfheartedly. "It was bloody awful. People in black masks tried to bury me alive. I was in an open wooden casket, and one by one these shrouded figures threw shovels of dirt on me. My hands were free, but I couldn't brush away the soil or climb out of the coffin. When I tried to shout for help, my voice was barely audible. No one heard me."

Paige smoothed out his tousled hair and kissed his brow. "What do you think it means?"

"I suppose I'm reacting to Gwen's death," replied Alec. "I felt so useless. I was right there and couldn't help her."

Paige shook her head in acknowledgement. "I think those kinds of nightmares spring from a person's desire to be in control. I know it's my nature to plan and prepare for every eventuality. But lately, I've come to realize, it's wiser to *let go* and trust that your life will unfold as it's intended."

A sense of normalcy began to return to Alec as he listened to Paige. She was right of course. Solving a murder case wasn't as simple as reconciling a bank account. It wasn't possible to predict the actions of others or even the outcome of your own efforts. There were just too many variables.

After a few minutes, Alec's eyes began to close and his breathing slowed. When he turned on his side, Paige whispered, "Do you think you can full back to sleep now?"

Alec's murmured reply was lost in the covers.

Paige wrapped her body around his. In a hushed voice, she said good night and kissed the nape of his neck.

Three hours later, the alarm clock jolted Alec awake. As usual, Paige was able to quickly silence the clamor while Alec tried to rouse himself. In no time at all, she called from the door, "I'll be right back with your cuppa."

Alec sighed as he watched Paige slip out of the room. In just eight days, Paige had helped him realize he was *more* than Shanna's husband and Emma's daddy. He felt that his newfound happiness was hanging by a thread and wondered whether he'd be able to relax once McGill interviewed her.

Paige reentered the room with Alec's mug and placed it on the nightstand. Before Alec could pull her into his waiting arms, she deftly moved away.

"I swear. You're like an octopus with eight sex-crazed tentacles. I have to be in the Churchill Room by seven thirty for disembarkation." Taking no chances, Paige blew him a kiss from the door and departed.

Getting twelve hundred vacationers off the Pegasus in a few hours was no small chore. The night before disembarkation the passengers were given color-coded luggage tags and numbers that correlated with their impending travel plans. The labels informed porters when and where to position the suitcases in the terminal building. The following morning, passengers waited in lounges throughout the ship listening for their numbers to be called. The system was used to prevent a frantic and dangerous exodus off the ship.

Most people found those final hours hectic. Many of them had planes to catch and some left just a few minutes to get to the airport. If they weren't rushing to make their connections, they dreaded the idea of returning to work. These formerly relaxed passengers left the cruise needing to go on another vacation.

Paige had been assigned to help handicapped passengers disembark. The policy of the cruise line was to assist the wheelchair-bound to the terminal building. Paige's job was to coordinate the staff members and make sure that there were enough wheelchairs to go around. She had assured Alec that she'd be finished with her duties well before her interview with McGill.

Alec met Douglas at the cargo ramp at 7:45 o'clock. The doctor looked tense waiting for the medical examiner's van to pick up Gwen's body. Even though Alec already knew the answer, he asked, "How are you doing?"

Douglas scowled. "I didn't sleep at all last night. I kept thinking I should have been better prepared. I felt so bleeding inadequate."

Alec shared those same sentiments, but tried to cheer up his friend. "You did what you could. There was no way for you to know what you were dealing with. We only suspected that Gwen was poisoned after I became ill."

At that moment, an official looking vehicle drove up to the security gate. The driver stopped to show the guard his papers and pulled up to the docking area. Douglas appeared to recognize him. While the young man approached them, he remarked, "I heard you had another one for me."

Alec couldn't help being reminded of Queen's ghoulish lyrics, "And another one gone, and another one gone, Another one bites the dust." As he watched Gwen's corpse being taken away, the verse repeated in his head.

Minutes later, McGill, his partner, and the forensics team joined them, and they proceeded to A Deck. En route, McGill asked whether the body had been picked up yet. Since the medical examiner was making her autopsy a priority, McGill expected to have the preliminary results before the ship sailed at 4:30.

Isa was in the corridor when they arrived and let the technicians into Gwen's cabin. He then led the rest of the group to the Dolphin Room. This time the lounge was well stocked with refreshments, other than coffee and cookies. There was a selection of fruit, assorted breads, and a platter of cold cuts and cheeses on the table. Alec thanked Isa, and McGill asked him to return with Widarta in thirty minutes. He wanted to get a full report from Alec and the doctor first.

McGill helped himself to several small Danishes, as his colleague arranged the room to his liking. Taking coffee from the urn, McGill confided to Alec, "I really enjoy conducting my interviews here. You know how to treat public servants."

After the detective swallowed his last bite, he turned on the tape recorder and asked Alec to describe Gwen's activities on the beach before she had showed signs of distress. Even though Alec briefed him yesterday on the phone, McGill needed to tape his statement so it could be transcribed onto paper and signed. Douglas followed Alec, and recounted in detail Gwen's physical symptoms and the medical protocol that was followed.

While the other detective was taking down the doctor's version, McGill asked Alec to retrieve Gwen's belongings from his office and bring them to the Dolphin Room. He wanted them at hand, so the criminologists could take them directly to the laboratory when they were finished. The sooner the suntan oil was analyzed, the sooner the case could be pursued in earnest.

Alec returned to the Dolphin Room to find that Isa and Widi had replaced Douglas. Both cabin stewards were seated at the table, enlightening the detectives about the daily habits of the officers and crewmembers on A Deck

On seeing Alec, McGill instructed his partner to take over for a while. He told Alec to leave Gwen's possessions in the corner of the room and to step out into the hall. Once they were a distance from the lounge, McGill bellowed, "Are you out of your damn mind? How could you sleep with Paige Anderson? You could have irreparably damaged *my* case."

Alec wasn't surprised that McGill found out. He was far more aggrieved by his tone and manner. Alec's features became stony as he replied curtly, "Look, I'm a British citizen, and I don't take orders from you! I haven't any proof that Paige is innocent, but I *know* she's incapable of murder. I hope you treat her with the respect she deserves when you speak to her."

McGill was taken aback for a moment and replied grudgingly, "As it happens, I don't consider her a suspect *at this time*. But, you took quite a chance. I looked through her personnel files and checked out her brother. After he was dismissed from your cruise line, Derek Anderson found a position at a top-notch hotel in San Francisco. Under those circumstances, I doubt Ms. Anderson would have remained embittered enough to murder Mark Linley."

While Alec was mulling over his words, McGill invited him to participate in the interviews as a "lie detector." The homicide detective specifically wanted him to listen to the suspects and tell him which ones were being untruthful.

When they returned to the room, McGill's associate told Alec where to sit. Those being interviewed were to have their back to the liaison officer. This way, McGill would be able to read Alec's expressions and gestures unhindered.

Alec took his place and started to speculate as to McGill's motives. Did McGill think he had something to do with Gwen's death? Why did the homicide detective give him such a hard time about his relationship with Paige, if she weren't a suspect? And more importantly, why did he still want to see Paige?

A few minutes after the cabin stewards departed, Scott Harris came to the door. While he remained in the hall, Alec told McGill about the cruise line's decision regarding his dismissal. In lieu of being criminally charged, Scott signed a note, promising to repay his debt over a ten-year period. The principal and interest amounted to over ten thousand dollars.

When Scott was permitted to enter the Dolphin Room, McGill asked him straight away, "What are your disembarkation plans today?"

Scott cleared his throat in a dignified fashion. "Eric Santos has asked me to stay with him for the time being. He lives in Miami Beach."

"Is he leaving the ship too?" queried McGill.

Scott looked uncomfortable and shifted his position slightly. "He has decided to seek employment elsewhere."

McGill smiled sarcastically and retorted, "Has he?"

For the next ten minutes, the detective grilled Scott. His description of the theft and denial of the murder echoed his previous statements. Scott said he knew nothing of Gwen's "illness," and had no contact with her while he was under house arrest.

Alec was surprised to learn that Scott was still dating Eric Santos. Since the men were planning to live together, it made Alec question Eric's alibi. Widarta had only seen Eric leave Scott's cabin late that morning. They could have killed Mark earlier when the cabin steward was working in the laundry.

McGill didn't seem too disturbed about their current relationship. He told Scott that he could leave the ship once Eric Santos signed a sworn affidavit confirming that he had been with the assistant controller from Saturday night to 7:00 the following morning. The homicide detective also wanted to know where they could be reached and directed them to provide a telephone number and an address.

Paige was scheduled next. She was told to wait outside the lounge while Santos signed the required documentation. When she was allowed in, McGill introduced himself and said, "I've been looking forward to meeting you."

Mystified, Paige turned to Alec as if to say, "What have you been telling him?"

Once they took their seats, McGill continued. "I understand that you worked on the Centaurus for a number of years. Can you tell me about Jeffrey Sheffield, the ship's plumber? I believe you and Linley served with him three years ago."

Alec had a tough time remaining silent during their exchange. He had no idea that Paige had known Jeffrey prior to sailing on the Pegasus. Suddenly, he felt betrayed and annoyed.

Paige twisted around and smiled weakly at Alec before replying. "I didn't want to get Jeffrey into trouble. He had an affair with Mark's assistant, Theresa, while he was married. In those days, Nora worked in a hospital in London. I don't know whether she ever learned of their romance. But, I've always suspected she joined the medical staff here to keep an eye on him."

The detective and Paige discussed Jeffrey's relationship with Mark while Alec reflected on Paige's remarks. Knowing how much she disliked Linley, Alec understood her reluctance to squeal on Jeffrey and distress Nora. It was also reasonable to conclude that Mark had been aware of Jeffrey's liaison with his former co-worker and tried to use it to his own advantage. When the meeting ended, McGill graciously thanked Paige and accompanied her to the door.

With Michelle Van Dam, McGill utilized a different interview technique. Alec noticed that he altered his speech pattern and asked shorter questions. From her answers, Alec's was able to confirm his assumptions about their relationship. Although Gwen and Michelle were outwardly civil to each other, they shared nothing in common. Michelle thought Gwen, in plain English, was a slut.

Since a common reception area connected the spas, McGill wanted to know whether Michelle had seen any of Gwen's "friends" come and go. Michelle rattled off several names. "There was Boyd, and Rick, and *him*." Michelle grinned as she looked behind her and pointed her finger straight at Alec. "Oh, I almost forgot. There was also that plumber. But, I haven't seen him since Christmas."

Gruffly, McGill asked, "Do you mean Jeffrey Sheffield?"

"I guess so, if he's the one who's married to the nurse."

Having heard Jeffrey's name now mentioned in two separate interviews, Alec wondered just how deeply he was involved. Did Gwen and Jeffrey have an affair?" Did Linley try to blackmail him? And did Jeffrey kill the controller and Gwen before either of them could tell Nora and ruin his marriage?

After Michelle was told she could go back to work, McGill left the room to check on the progress of the crime scene investigators. Shortly later, he returned with them. As they carried away Gwen's personal effects, the detective reminded them to call as soon as they had *any* information.

With no appointments until one, the three men broke for lunch. Alec led the detectives to the Deli Bar on the Lido Deck, and discovered that McGill's silent partner had a name. It was Garret McHale. Alec smiled, imagining what their fellow officers called them when they were out of hearing range.

Seated near the pool, they gobbled down sandwiches of corned beef and pastrami, and drank huge quantities of iced tea. McGill candidly spoke about the investigation and told Alec he was pleased to uncover a new suspect. He hadn't expected to learn anything worthwhile until the suntan oil was analyzed and the autopsy completed.

Over their meal, Alec asked McGill what happened with the passengers who had been audited by Mark Linley while he was employed with the Internal Revenue Service. McGill laughed sheepishly and told Alec that it turned out to be a waste of time. He and McHale flew all the way to Chicago to find out that the man was frail and in his eighties. His wife was no better off and could barely lift up the percolator to pour them coffee. Alec was glad to know that even professionals made mistakes occasionally.

The afternoon promised to be more hectic than the morning. Ronald Bauer, Rick Tanner, and Boyd Griffin, had appointments. McGill also wanted to add the male fitness director and Jeffrey Sheffield to his list. Unfortunately, Alec wasn't able to contact either of them during lunch.

Just as they returned to the Dolphin Room, McGill's cell phone rang. He answered it, indicating to McHale that he had the medical examiner on the line.

McGill's responded, "Are you certain? That definitely puts a whole new spin on her death. Have them test it against Mark Linley's DNA. And get back to me when you isolate the poison."

After the detective finished with his call, he looked up expectantly.

Alec and McHale waited anxiously for McGill to spill the beans. Finally, Alec yelled, "Well, what did he say?"

Smiling, as though he'd won the lottery, he replied, "Apparently, your fitness instructor was three months pregnant!"

CHAPTER 12

▼

"LIVE TO TELL"

Words & Music—Madonna Ciccone & Pat Leonard

Wednesday Afternoon—1ˢᵗ of February

It took Alec a moment for McGill's statement to sink in. Alec didn't like to speak ill of the dead, but he thought quite a few men on the Pegasus could have impregnated Gwen. Counting backwards, Alec concluded that she conceived at the beginning of November. Rick, Boyd, and Jeffrey, had all been on the ship since mid October when the Southern Dreams' Tour got underway.

For the next several minutes, the men discussed the ramifications of Gwen's pregnancy on the case. Even though her "big news" had probably been unexpected, Alec couldn't imagine her distraught enough to commit suicide. On Monday night, she sounded overjoyed to be marring Boyd and moving to New York City.

They also debated whether Gwen killed Mark to keep him from exposing her secret. But that left three questions. Did Mark Linley know about Gwen's pregnancy; would she care; and who murdered Gwen? To Alec, it appeared most likely that Rick or Jeffrey permanently silenced her in the mistaken belief it would conceal her pregnancy. There was also a slim chance that her pregnancy had nothing to do with her death or Mark's.

Recalling that McGill mentioned Mark's name on the phone, Alec asked in disbelief, "You don't think that she and Linley had a fling, do you?"

"I doubt it, but we have his DNA on hand and you never know. Speaking of DNA," McGill turned to McHale, "Do we have enough mouth swabs?"

His partner peered into his briefcase and gave him the thumbs up sign. McGill went on to explain to Alec that he could obtain DNA from volunteers, but would need a court order to compel those who refused. Since the test wasn't physically intrusive, Alec hoped Boyd Griffin would undergo the procedure. The results would either confirm his paternity or point to others.

At one o'clock, the second round of interviews began In the light of recent events, Alec wasn't sure whether to include Bauer in his list of suspects. He didn't appear to have the temperament of a killer, and Alec couldn't see him interested in Gwen or any woman for that matter. Moreover, McGill wasn't able to find a reason for Bauer's hostility toward the controller, even though he seemed intent on having him sacked.

While McGill invited Bauer to take a seat, Alec walked over to *his* chair in the corner of the lounge. Alec noticed that the room looked tidy again. The cabin stewards had cleaned away the uneaten food and discarded dishes. In the center of the table a tray of little cakes and fruit tartlets now stood, beckoning Alec's taste buds. Still sated from lunch, Alec decided he would treat himself later.

Soon after McHale started to record the proceedings, McGill asked the security officer why he reported Linley's behavior to headquarters. Bauer replied that Mark was an "intolerable bully," and he felt crew morale would improve once he was dismissed. Alec could find no fault with his logic.

During the rest of the interview, McGill and the security officer discussed Gwen. McGill wanted to know whether she'd ever been "written up" for improper behavior, and who had access to her cabin. To those questions, he replied, "She had a clean record, and only Isa and my staff have pass keys."

After hearing the last exchange, Alec began to ask himself *how* and *when* the poisoned suntan oil found its way into Gwen's possession. Just last night, Rick Tanner tried to get into Gwen's room. Did he want to retrieve a damaging piece of evidence? It would have been easy for any of her so-called beaus to tamper with her belongings. Alec wasn't surprised to hear McGill ask Bauer, "How many keys were issued to Ms. Llewelyn?"

Obligingly, the chief of security responded, "I'll check with the front desk. If a key is reported lost or stolen, the staff is supposed to change the computerized door code and issue a new card on the spot. I'm certain a duplicate would not have been given out without written authorization from Gwen."

The detective nodded, "When you get that information, please give it directly to Mr. DunBarton."

As Bauer was preparing to leave, McGill asked him whether he'd mind taking a DNA test. The security officer looked as though he was going to say *no* when he glanced at Alec. A moment later, he agreed.

While McHale swabbed the inside of Bauer's cheek, Alec speculated as to why he submitted to the procedure. Did he think that Alec was going to report him to the captain for being uncooperative? More importantly, why didn't Bauer ask the detective why he wanted his DNA?

Rick Tanner was next. Alec was eager to see McGill handle the cruise director. Regrettably, he never got the chance. Rick glared at Alec when he stepped into the room and declared, "I don't want DunBarton here. If he stays, I'll sue *you* and your asinine department!"

McGill walked Alec to the hall and gave him a wink. "I promise to fill you in later. In the meantime, see whether you can round up the plumber and fitness director." Before going back inside, the detective smiled sadistically and said, "I'm gonna enjoy my little chat with Tanner."

Alec was astonished to see how many new passengers had boarded the ship in the last few hours. Many of them were in the gym, enthusiastically trying out fitness equipment. Hoping to spot Zack, Alec glanced around the room and noticed that Gwen's 8x10 inch photo no longer stood on the counter. While he was mourning its sudden disappearance, a young woman came up behind him. Alec realized she was Gwen's replacement after seeing the familiar insignia on her shirt pocket.

He soon learned her name was Jillian, and she had just finished an eight-month stint on the Aquarius. She had been home in Boston for two weeks when the cruise line called her late last night and implored her to join the Pegasus.

Cognizant of his limited time, Alec quickly explained that he needed to talk to Zack. At the mention of his name, the young woman smiled like a cat that swallowed a canary, and purred, "He left a few minutes ago to grab something to eat."

Zack was seated at a small table near the pool, munching on a burger when Alec approached him. Seeing the liaison officer, he inquired, "How's Gwen doing? I heard she's in the hospital with appendicitis."

Not sure how to respond, Alec merely said, "They're taking good care of her." Alec briefly told Zack that his presence was required in the Dolphin Room. Since Boyd was to follow Tanner, Alec told him to get there at 3:00 P.M. He seemed a bit perplexed, but agreed to meet Alec and McGill at the designated time.

Tracking down Jeffrey was another matter. Since lunch, Alec had been paging him with no results. Certain Douglas would have some information, Alec set off for the infirmary.

The doctor and Maggie were in the middle of logging in recently delivered medical supplies when Alec arrived slightly out of breath. Douglas left her to finish on her own and bid Alec into his inner sanctum. As he shut the door, he said, "I see you've been exerting yourself. What's going on with McGill?"

"Quite a bit. But right now I have to find Jeffrey Sheffield. Do you know where he is?"

Douglas glimpsed at his wristwatch. "He and Nora left here several hours ago. They went into Fort Lauderdale. They should be back four thirtyish. Does McGill want to see him? He can't possibly be involved in Gwen's death!"

Before Alec turned to leave, he teased, "A lot you know! I'll bring you up to date this evening. Can you meet me and Paige at the sail-away party?"

"I'll be there with bells on," replied Douglas with a curious expression.

Alec returned to the Dolphin Room to find Boyd waiting in the corridor. His expression was somber and served to remind Alec that Mark Linley and Gwen Llewelyn were not the killer's only victims. Just as Alec was about to ask Boyd how he was doing, Rick flew out of the lounge in a rage.

On seeing Alec, Tanner stopped and spat, "You're a real bastard." Alec was taken aback by his vehemence, but couldn't wait to hear what caused his outburst.

Even though McGill was chuckling when Alec and Boyd entered the room, he resumed his poker face within seconds. Once they were all seated, McGill extended his condolences to Boyd on his recent loss. After their polite exchange, the detective's first question had a cold ring to it.

On being asked about his relationship with Gwen, Boyd glanced at Alec and then returned his attention to the detective. Appearing confused, he blurted out, "Why are you asking me about Gwen? Mr. DunBarton told me she died from a respiratory illness. Was it something else? Was she murdered?"

McGill nodded. "We haven't received the autopsy results yet, but we strongly suspect that her suntan oil was laced with poison."

Boyd cried, "That son of a bitch killed her! I'm sure of it."

Talking more slowly, he continued. "Weeks ago, Gwen told me she was pregnant. She didn't know who was responsible and decided to get an abortion in St. Maarten last Thursday. While waiting at the clinic, she had a change of heart and didn't go through with it. The next evening, she told Rick he might be the baby's father. He became furious with Gwen and threatened to kill her if she ruined his plans to marry Janet Kane."

"Weren't you angry, she'd been with other men," snapped McGill.

Suddenly Boyd looked very tired. "Look, Gwen had a lot of problems. As a kid, her uncle sexually abused her. She often did things on impulse and used sex as a way to get what she wanted. When Gwen was hurt or lonely, she'd transfer her affections from one man to another. She had finally begun to trust me, and now she's dead."

During the next twenty minutes, it was revealed that Boyd also knew of Gwen's "friendship" with Jeffrey Sheffield. According to him, Gwen stopped seeing the plumber a couple of months ago. It was right after Nora paid her a visit.

When Boyd was asked whether Mark could have known about her condition, he replied, "I don't think it's possible. Gwen took one of those at-home pregnancy tests the morning she found his body in the gym. She had never been very regular and only began to think she was pregnant when she started to have morning sickness."

At the close of the interview, the detective asked Boyd whether he'd take a DNA test to establish paternity. Boyd readily agreed and acknowledged that the issue had been troubling him for some time. As McHale set out the paraphernalia, McGill came over to Alec and whispered, "What do you think?"

Alec couldn't see Boyd as a cold-blooded killer. From reading murder mysteries, Alec had gathered that poison was largely a women's weapon. With Nora Sheffield now in the picture, Alec decided she was a far more likely suspect.

Once the specimen was enclosed in a plastic bag and labeled, Boyd rose to go. Before leaving the lounge, McGill warned, "I'll want to see you when the ship returns to port on the 10th."

Alec was about to ask McGill about his meeting with Rick Tanner when Zack arrived. McGill's session with the fitness instructor proceeded smoothly. He merely told Zack that he was looking into Gwen's relationship with Mark. The detective questioned him about Gwen's male visitors and her behavior in general. Since Zack had only been on the Pegasus a short time, he could only attest to seeing her with Boyd and Alec.

As to her moods, he remembered that she was very pleased with herself on Saturday when she announced that she'd be coming into some money. When Zack asked her how, Gwen simply smiled.

After hearing that disclosure, McGill and Alec gazed at each other, appearing to be asking themselves the same questions. Did Gwen witness the murder or find evidence in the gym that identified the killer? Did she try to blackmail Linley's murderer? Or did she merely expect Rick to foot the bill for her maternity expenses. Since Gwen planned to keep the baby, and Boyd had not yet proposed, it was a possibility.

McGill concluded his inquiry by asking Zack about her daily habits. When the fitness instructor remarked that she worked out daily and sunbathed at the seawater pool, Alec began to recall the day he went swimming with Gwen.

As soon as Zack left the room, Alec exclaimed, "I can't believe it slipped my mind. Gwen kept her tanning supplies in a tote bag in the gym. Anyone using the spa facilities could have gotten to them easily.

"On the day we went to the pool, Gwen had two bottles of suntan oil. One was nearly empty. If the poison was in the full bottle, she could have been carrying it around for weeks!"

The detective nodded and agreed with Alec's conclusions.

In the remaining time before the Pegasus was due to sail, McGill phoned the laboratory to see how the chemical analysis was coming along. When he hung up, he told Alec that the technicians had several more tests to run. He expected that they'd be finished in a few more hours.

Before disembarking, the detective instructed Alec to question both Jeffrey and Nora Sheffield. Alec, in turn, gave McGill his cabin number and asked him call him as soon as the results were in.

Just as Alec waved goodbye to the detectives, the passenger lifeboat drill was announced. To Alec, the sound of the horns, not only signified a beginning of another cruise, but also new life to the case. Even though, he had more questions than answers, Alec felt optimistic that Gwen would speak from the grave. As Madonna wrote in her song, "The secret I have learned, 'till then, It will burn inside of me." Was it possible that her corpse would "live to tell" it secrets?

At half past five, Alec, Paige, and Douglas gathered at a small table on the Lido Deck to observe the sail-away celebration below. From his vantage point, Alec was able to watch the passengers enjoy their departure from Port Everglades.

On his first trip out, Alec missed the event since he was at the captain's meeting being introduced as the Liaison Officer. This time there would be no get-together. Only a few crewmembers knew Gwen was dead, and Jarvis wanted to keep it that way.

After they were served their drinks, they watched Rick introduce his dependable staff to the partygoers. By now Alec was familiar with most of the faces. The only one he didn't recognize was Faith, the assistant cruise director, who directed the activities of the children from a high tech "club-house" on the Sun Deck.

When the festivities ended and the musicians began to wrap up, it was finally quiet enough to tell Douglas and Paige about his day.

At first, Paige reacted with surprise to the news of Gwen's pregnancy and then confided, "I should have realized it! A couple of weeks ago, I ran into her in the ladies' room. She was in dreadful shape and couldn't stop vomiting. Gwen told me she had too much to drink. It didn't occur to me at the time, but she never touched anything stronger than diet cola."

Douglas added, "Gwen asked me if I knew of any decent doctors on the islands. She told me that her IUD was causing a problem. I was so relieved she didn't ask me to take a look at it, I gave her the names of several gyne-cologists."

It amazed Alec how much each of them knew individually. Gazing at his two dearest friends, Alec chastised, "From this moment on, you're to tell me *everything* you know about the people involved in this case! I don't care if your information is five years old or you're trying to protect some-one's privacy. There's a killer on this ship, and I'm not certain the murder spree is over. Do I make myself clear?"

Paige turned beet red and muttered an apology while the doctor replied solemnly, "My dear boy, you're right of course. I promise to keep you informed."

"Good, we have that settled."

"Speaking of murder suspects," Alec continued, "Rick Tanner called me a bastard after his interview with McGill."

Paige gasped. "I saw him just an hour ago with his fiancée Janet. She's on this cruise, you know. When they were going into his office, I overheard him say he has it in for someone on the ship. Oh Alec, did he mean you?"

Alec nodded. "I'm afraid I've put his knickers in a twist. Though, I have no idea what I did. He tolerated me on Thursday and hated me by Saturday. Maybe he thinks I talked Gwen out of having the abortion."

Deciding it was a good time to change the subject, Alec said, "My stomach is growling. Why don't we step into the restaurant for dinner?"

As they stood on line, Paige nudged Alec's arm. "Look over my shoulder, but don't stare. That woman with Rick is Janet Kane."

Since hearing varying descriptions of Janet, Alec was eager to see Tanner's fiancée. Douglas had not exaggerated about her looks. She was delicate and petite with large doe eyes and dark brown hair that hung in ringlets to her shoulders. Even from a distance, Alec had to admit she was stunning.

At eight o'clock, Alec and Paige returned to his stateroom hoping that McGill had called with the information. Frustrated that the message light on the telephone wasn't blinking, Alec decided to take a shower.

The call came through as Alec turned the off the faucet. In response to Paige's shout, Alec emerged from the bathroom wrapped up in a towel. While he shook the excess water from his hair, he took the receiver from Paige.

Alec listened for a couple of minutes before speaking. Finally, he said, "Is it common? Where would I find it?" Just before hanging up, he exclaimed, "That much!" As Alec placed the phone back in its cradle, he felt remarkably energized.

Paige joined him as he was concluding his conversation. "How much of what?"

Alec smiled at her and said, "Nicotine."

"The nicotine in cigarettes?"

"Well, sort of. This nicotine came from a patch."

"The patch?"

"You know, those giant band aids of nicotine. They sell it to people who want to quit smoking."

"Was it in her suntan oil?"

"Aye. Her bottle contained the equivalent of sixty patches. McGill said that's almost 1,300 milligrams of nicotine. A heavy smoker can tolerate sixty milligrams in a twenty-four hour period and a nonsmoker considerably less. Gwen received hers all at once. The poor kid never had a chance!"

CHAPTER 13

▼

"YOU'RE THE TOP"

Words & Music—Cole Porter

Thursday Morning—2nd of February

After learning that Gwen died from nicotine poisoning, it took Alec hours to fall asleep. Despite his lack of shuteye, Alec woke up early the next day. By six thirty, he was fully dressed and sprawled out on the shabby leather couch in the Dolphin Lounge. A number of books were scattered at his feet. Alec was on a mission to find out all he could about nicotine. McGill just didn't give him enough information on the phone.

At first, Alec was actually disappointed that the Pegasus carried one of the newer editions of *Encyclopedia Britannica*. When he was a lad, the volumes ran from A to Zed. There was no micropaedia, macropedia, or propaedia to fiddle around with. It was in the micropaedia that Alec located "nicotine." Predominantly interested in the symptoms of an overdose, he learned that nicotine was "a highly toxic poison that causes vomiting and nausea, stomach pains, and in severe cases, convulsions, paralysis, and death." Alec felt he could attest to that.

As he scanned down the page, Alec read that nicotine was also an effective agent in insecticides. It amazed him that such a lethal substance could be such an integral part of his cherished pipe tobacco.

Even though Alec found related articles in the "knowledge in depth" section, he decided to go online to widen his search. Since traces of adhesives were also discovered in the suntan oil, McGill and his team were quite certain that the poison was leached from the non-smoking aid.

From one website, Alec gleaned several riveting facts about nicotine patches. Under "adverse reactions," the report stated that a lethal *oral* dose in non-smoking adults was close to fifty milligrams and that skin absorption was even more virulent. Since the killer chose a bizarre way to poison Gwen, Alec began to hypothesize what the murderer may have known. Did he or she research the topic carefully or was it happenstance that Gwen received the fatal dosage?

As Alec replaced the encyclopedias back in the bookcase, he decided to pay a visit to the doctor. Over dinner, Douglas asked him to keep him informed. Because it was still early, Alec called his stateroom first.

On hearing, "Doctor Abbot here," Alec inquired, "Is that you?"

Recognizing his Scottish brogue, Douglas retorted, "Who else would it be?" He added with some urgency in his voice, "There's nothing wrong, is there? You're usually dead to the world at this time of the day."

"Speaking of dead, I found out what caused Gwen's death. Are you up for some breakfast or are you needed in surgery?"

A minute later, Alec was at the doctor's cabin waiting for him to turn off his lights and snatch his key. While Douglas was shutting his door, he demanded, "Well, what was it?"

Making sure that no one was within hearing range, Alec gravely responded, "Nicotine poisoning."

For a few moments, Douglas looked baffled. Slowly, he began to shake his head and show a glimmer of comprehension. "That would make sense. I believe that nicotine is an alkaloid, which causes respiratory paralysis and cardiovascular collapse."

Over breakfast, Alec filled him in. When Douglas was told that Gwen's eight-ounce bottle of suntan oil contained nearly 1,300 milligrams of nicotine, he whistled and remarked, "The killer planned it perfectly."

"Who would come up with such an idea?" Alec wondered aloud.

The doctor explained that smokers who bought the patch would receive a written disclosure in each packet specifying the risks of overdose. Since the medicine no longer required a prescription, it was available to almost anyone, anywhere.

Alec told Douglas that the detectives planned to review the credit card transactions of the suspects in hope of finding someone who had purchased the patches.

Taking a leaf from his book, Alec decided to examine the sales receipts of the ship's boutique and duty-free shop to learn which crewmembers bought suntan oil and nicotine products during the last few months.

Douglas agreed it would be a good idea, and then glanced down at his wristwatch to check the time.

Suddenly a melodic voice behind Alec chanted, "You're not planning to leave, are you? I was hoping we could renew our friendship."

Alec turned his head and glanced up at the lady who took the doctor's breath away. It was Janet Kane. Before he could stop himself, Alec audibly sang out, "You're the top! You're the…Mona Lisa. You're the top! You're the Tower of Pisa."

Although Alec didn't get the words right, Janet beamed in response to his tribute. He, in turn blushed, thinking he ought to be more judicious with a passenger and possible killer.

Douglas got to his feet and helped her transfer her bagel and coffee from her tray to the table.

Trying to dignify the proceedings, the doctor eloquently stated, "Alec, I'd like you to meet Janet Kane. Janet, this singing minstrel is Alec Dun-Barton, an old friend of mine. He's currently serving on the Pegasus as our Liaison Officer."

After they took their seats, Janet gave Alec an endearing smile. "I've heard that you're investigating the murders of Mark Linley and Gwen Llewelyn."

Getting over his earlier embarrassment, Alec returned her smile with a charming one of his own and asked, "How did you find out about Gwen? It's pretty hush-hush here on the ship."

Lowering her voice, she replied, "Oh, please excuse my faux pas. I should have realized it's not common knowledge. Rick, my fiancé, told me in confidence. Have you any idea what caused her death?"

Before Alec could respond, Douglas rose and explained, "I'm terribly sorry I can't stay. I'm needed in the infirmary shortly." As he clasped Janet's hand, he added, "It's always so good to see you my dear. I hope we can have a quiet conversation later on."

When Douglas released his grasp, Alec noticed the engagement ring that had mesmerized Beth Romano on the evening before Linley's death. Interested in having a better look, Alec asked, "May I see your diamond? I hear it's spectacular."

As the doctor slipped away, Janet regally placed her hand on Alec's palm. His attention was drawn to one particular prong that seemed higher than the others. Viewing the brilliant stone, he could understand why Gwen felt so dejected when she saw Janet's ring.

Alec enjoyed his conversation with Ms. Kane. She told him about her whirlwind romance with Rick and their plans to wed in April. Even though Alec would have liked to advise her *not* to marry the cruise director, he held his tongue. From speaking to her, he realized she was quite astute and strong willed. For a moment, he wondered whether he ought to warn Tanner instead. Alec was doubtful she'd put up with his nonsense.

After Janet finished her breakfast, Alec walked her to the elevator. She told him that she was going to Coral Cay for a back massage on the beach. Being wrapped up in Gwen's murder, Alec forgot that the even-numbered cruises landed at their ports-of-call in the opposite order. He said a hurried goodbye to Janet as the elevator doors shut and continued on to the shopping arcade.

Several hours later, Alec was seated in his office, scowling at a stack of daily sales logs. Alec recognized the names of four crewmembers who had purchased Cruisin' Coconut, Gwen's brand of suntan oil. There was Jeffrey Sheffield, Rick Tanner, Paige Anderson, and Michelle Van Dam. Alec was upset to see Paige's name and cabin number listed on the statement from the boutique.

It seemed to Alec that God or the fates didn't want him to feel too secure in his relationship with Paige. Alec found some consolation in learning that Michelle bought the product also. She was nearly as pale as the chief of security. It begged the question, "Why did she spend money on something she obviously never used?"

Since that Pegasus did not sell nonsmoking aids, such as the patch, inhalers, or nicotine chewing gums, Alec's only recourse was to examine cigarette and cigar sales on the ship. Douglas was right. Smokers would be more aware of the toxicity of nicotine if they had tried to quit at onetime or another.

Many of the ship's staff members obtained cigarettes from the duty-free shop on board. Rick Tanner, Jeffrey Sheffield, and Ronald Bauer were among them. Although it was rather unusual for cigar smokers to inhale and become as addicted to nicotine as their counterparts, Alec checked those who procured fine cigars. Captain Jarvis and Dr. Abbot were part of that exclusive group.

For a crazy moment, Alec wondered whether his good friend could have cold-bloodedly murdered two people. The thought *almost* made him laugh.

A knock at the door interrupted Alec's musings. He was rather startled to see the captain in the outer office with an elderly female officer who had evidently just joined the Pegasus.

"I'm pleased you're here, Alec," said Jarvis. "I'd like to present you to Regina Hill, our new Assistant Controller. She used to work in our New York office, and for the last five years has served on the Monoceros. Ms. Hill, meet Alec DunBarton, our Liaison Officer."

Before the captain departed, he directed Alec to show Regina around the ship.

Alec hailed, "Welcome aboard," as the office door shut behind Jarvis.

In turn, Regina grinned and exclaimed, "What in the world is going on here? And what does a liaison officer do?"

Alec laughed heartily. He could tell straight away that he and Regina would get along well. While Regina became acclimated to her new workspace, Alec briefly told her about the murders, and his role in the investigation as the auditor, and eyes and ears of the police department.

She listened attentively and then declared, "Oh, please let me help you. I'm tougher than I look, and I do love a good mystery."

Observing her bright blue eyes sparkle in determination, Alec was instantly reminded of one of his favorite old-time actresses, Helen Hayes, who had played the role of Agatha Christie's Miss Marple quite a few times. Regina was about five feet tall and a bit plump. Her gray hair was arranged in a French knot that sat neatly on the top of her head. She possessed an ageless quality that Alec found very appealing.

To show off the Pegasus, Alec decided it would be best to start on the Sun Deck and work down. Regina appeared delighted to have a young, handsome officer point out the hot spots. Alec gallantly offered her his arm, and they began the grand tour.

After exploring the upper promenade Alec suggested lunch. Over their meal, Alec found out that Regina had been born and raised in the Lake District of England. As a young woman, she was an idealist and joined the Peace Corps in the 1960's.

With a great deal of tenderness, Regina explained how she met her husband, an American engineer. They saw a good part of world and settled down in Long Island to raise a family. When Regina's husband died suddenly from a brain embolism, she took a position at cruise headquarters. On her sixtieth birthday, Regina felt ready for adventure and transferred to the Monoceros. While Alec listened to her, he realized that she wasn't just a survivor, but also a woman who feasted on life.

Somewhat later, Alec and Regina reached the infirmary on the Marine Deck, the lowest passenger deck. When they walked into the room, the doctor strode over to Ms. Hill. In a cultured and solicitous voice, Douglas asked, "How may I help you?"

Alec smiled to himself, thinking that his approach only lacked a bow from the waist and a kiss on the hand.

As he introduced them, Alec wondered whether Janet Kane was losing her number one spot on Douglas's hit parade. After the three chatted a few minutes, they made plans to meet for drinks in the Zodiac Bar at eight.

Noticing the time, Alec and Regina took their leave. At 4:00 P.M., Regina was scheduled to meet with the Guest Relations Manager who had filed the corporate reports for Scott Harris while he was incarcerated.

After Regina picked up the papers from the front desk, Alec accompanied her back to their office, promising to see her later that evening.

Having reached a dead end in his nicotine inquires, Alec decided to hunt for Bauer and find out just how many door keys were issued to Gwen. Since it was still teatime, Alec paid a visit to the security officer's favorite haunt—the Churchill Room.

In the quiet lounge, Alec was rewarded by the sight of Officer Bauer having a cozy tête-à-tête with Michelle Van Dam. Alec liked to pretend that nothing shocked him, but this time, he was truly astounded. Bauer seemed to be a man *in love*.

Michelle was animated and chattering happily. Alec wished he could overhear their conversation, but the rattle of cups and saucers made eavesdropping very difficult. Instead, he watched from a large potted plant and hoped that he wouldn't be observed. Alec was too husky a man to remain hidden for long.

Minutes later, Michelle got up from the table and whispered something in Bauer's ear. The security officer smiled in response and was just about to rise from his seat when Alec passed by nonchalantly. Pretending to see the officer for the first time, Alec said, "I'm glad I've run into you. Were you able to get that list for me?"

Glancing at the recently vacated table, he slyly added, "Oh, I trust I'm not taking you away from your friend."

"No, we were finished," he mumbled. "Why don't you follow me to my office? I have what you need."

Along the way, Bauer asked Alec about Gwen's autopsy results. Not ready to disclose that information, Alec shook his head and said, "McGill will let me know when the laboratory has concluded its investigation. I'll keep you posted."

The list from the front office turned out to be nothing. According to the record book, Gwen applied for a duplicate key on the14th of January and never reported a lost or stolen card. The lack of information didn't particularly disturb Alec since he felt certain that the poisoned suntan oil found its way into Gwen's tote bag at the fitness center.

With all the talk of duplicate keys, Alec realized that Paige should have access to his cabin. They were growing closer everyday, and she needed to be able to get into his stateroom.

At the Front Desk, Alec obtained a second card after signing the authorization form. Indecisive how to spend the rest of the afternoon, he returned to his room to rest and page the plumber. Alec didn't have to wait long for a return call. When he picked up the receiver, Sheffield said with a chuckle, "It's your helpful handyman. What have *you* flushed down your toilet?"

Alec responded in kind. "I'll have you know, my loo is just fine. I was hoping we could meet tomorrow. McGill wanted me to ask you a few questions."

There was a pause before Jeffrey replied, "I can meet you at the Bull Dog Pub at, say about, three?"

"That would be great," agreed Alec. When he hung up, he realized that his attitude toward the plumber had changed. Although he enjoyed his company the other evening, Alec had grave misgivings about his character.

Alec and Paige were the first to arrive in the Zodiac Bar and watched for Douglas and Regina to arrive. Alec's eyes twinkled gaily as he told Paige about the captivating new assistant controller. Though he gave her the salient details of Regina's life, he omitted one important fact—her age.

Paige was in the midst of telling Alec about the inauguration of a new Flagship cruise ship when he spied Douglas making his way to their table. Seeing them alone, Douglas asked, "What, no Regina?"

Paige looked a bit put out and protested, "Not you too?"

Alec was touched and amused by her display of jealousy.

Regina showed up just as Alec was ordering two gin and tonics and a Glenlivet from the waiter.

Tucking an unruly wisp of hair in her bun, Regina said, "Make that two."

Alec grinned as the doctor graciously stood up and held out her chair. He was delighted that Douglas now seemed interested in a mature woman with a discriminating palate.

While Paige and Regina were being introduced to each other, Alec received a swift kick to his shin. When Alec grimaced in pain, Paige attempted to hide her smile.

Addressing herself to Regina, Paige said, "It's very nice to meet you. You've made quite an impression on these gentlemen."

"Oh, stuff and nonsense," replied Regina, appearing pleased to be part of the small group.

Over drinks, Regina told them how corporate headquarters operated and about her last few years on the Monoceros. The doctor entertained them with stories about some of his outlandish patients, and Paige laughed as she repeated one of those silly questions that passengers often asked. The woman wanted to know whether "the crew slept on board."

Once the laughter subsided, Alec began to tell them about seeing Bauer in the Churchill Room with a female staff member. At the mention of his name, Regina began to choke on her drink. While Douglas gently patted her back, Regina gasped, "Do you mean Ronald Bauer, the chief of security?"

Suddenly, all eyes were upon her. Alec asked hurriedly, "How do you know him?"

"Officer Bauer was on the Monoceros a few years ago," Regina explained. "He had quite a thing for a young massage therapist—a short blonde girl from South Africa. He followed her around like a puppy dog. I believe she later reported him to the captain, and he was asked to transfer to another ship. It was all rather odd."

Unable to contain himself any longer, Alec blurted, "Was her name Michelle Van Dam?"

Regina looked at Alec shrewdly. "Yes, I believe it was."

CHAPTER 14

▼

"HANDY MAN"

Words & Music—Otis Blackwell & Jimmy Jones

Thursday Evening—2nd of February

After Douglas and Regina retired for the evening, Alec and Paige went for a walk along the Promenade Deck. It was a misty night, and the weather added to Alec's restlessness. Two questions were uppermost in his mind. He needed to find out how long Bauer had been pursuing Michelle, and when she begin to welcome his advances. Now, it seemed clear why the chief of security wanted to get rid of Mark Linley.

Paige listened to Alec's ramblings as they briskly circled the wooden walkway. In some places the promenade was wet and slippery, and not many passengers were out and about. Noticing that Paige was having difficulty keeping up with him, Alec slowed down and asked, "Would you like to take a break for a minute?"

Smiling, Paige said, "I'm exhausted. You seem to be a man possessed."

While Alec was transferring cushions from the storage bin to the plastic lounge chairs, he commented, "I don't think I'm the only one who's possessed. Douglas seems smitten with our Regina."

"Do you think he wants to *see* her?"

"I'll find out more when I meet him for breakfast tomorrow. I hope he won't be as difficult as I was when I fell for you!"

Alec sat down and patted his thigh, inviting Paige to sit on his lap. Paige took a seat on the empty deck chair instead and objected, "No way, Mister. I just remembered; I'm very angry with you. How could you tease me so mercilessly?"

Undaunted Alec learned over and began to kiss her neck. Seeing goose bumps emerge on Paige's arm, Alec continued his onslaught until his body was perched on the side of his lounge chair. Observing his awkward position, she asked, "Are you ready for bed now?"

Alec smiled sheepishly as Paige rose from her seat. Saucily, she added, "You seem to be."

Alec rushed over to the table where Douglas was eating his breakfast. "Sorry I'm late. Were you waiting long?"

"No, not too long. Were have you been?"

"I'll tell you in a minute. First, I have to get something to eat." When he returned, he had French toast, sausages, and a cup of coffee.

"So, why were you delayed or shouldn't I ask?"

"Oh, get your mind out of the gutter. If you must know, I was in the health spa. I made arrangements to meet Michelle at eleven. What do you think Bauer is up to?"

Douglas shrugged. "I've never been able to figure him out. He's so nondescript. I didn't even know he was interested in the fairer sex."

The doctor's expression then changed from one of ennui to elation. "Regina is very special. Don't you think so?"

Alec smiled in reply. "What happened after you left the Zodiac Bar?"

"I walked Regina to her cabin. She's now in Mark Linley's old stateroom. The captain will be introducing her tonight at the welcome receptions along with Paige and myself. I've asked her join us for dinner."

"That will be grand," agreed Alec.

During their meal, they discussed the Sheffields. Alec wanted to know whether the doctor had ever seen Nora angry with or jealous of Gwen. Douglas seemed reluctant to answer, but he admitted that Nora had a temper. He recalled that she accused Jeffrey of flirting with Beth Romano seven months ago when the ship was in Alaska, following the Northern

Dreams' itinerary. The quarrel took place right after Nora miscarried for a second time.

While Douglas talked about new fertility treatments, Alec wondered whether Nora knew of Gwen's pregnancy. If she thought her husband had fathered a child with another woman, she might have become homicidal.

That would explain a motive to murder Gwen. Would she have killed Mark to keep her husband's affair quiet? According to Paige, Mark had been aware of Jeffrey's adulterous behavior on the Centaurus. Knowing the controller's penchant for blackmail, Mark would have welcomed news of Jeffrey's ongoing infidelity on the Pegasus.

Douglas impatiently stabbed Alec in the shoulder with his coffee spoon. "Well, what do you think?"

"Think about what?"

"Where have you been? I wanted to know if I should tell my daughter, I met a nice woman."

Alec had been pondering whether Nora and Jeffrey could have acted together in murdering Mark and Gwen, while Douglas was worrying that his forty-year old daughter would mind that he wanted to "date" again.

Good naturedly Alec responded, "Why don't you wait and see how this evening goes? Regina may have other ideas."

As Alec uttered those words, the doctor's face fell. There was nothing he could say after that remark to restore Douglas's high spirits.

After spending several hours searching the ship for a master copy of the plumbing log, Alec was happy to relax and wait for Michelle in the spa reception area. Before meeting Jeffrey at two, Alec wanted to know just how many times Gwen reported a blockage in her "pipes." He also needed to crosscheck his copy of the repair log against the original. Trusting Sheffield to do it, was like asking a wolf to guard a hen house.

The lyrics to the James Taylor's song "Handy Man," came to mind as Alec thought about the plumber. In a Scottish accent, Alec began to croon, "If your broken heart needs repair, I'm the man to see, I whisper sweet things, you tell all your friends. They come runnin' to me." It seemed to fit Jeffrey's modus operandi perfectly.

Watching Michelle walk toward him, Alec wondered what song summarized Officer Bauer's activities. Until he knew any different, "Every Breath You Take" by Sting appeared to be the most appropriate song for a stalker.

Eager to have a word with her, Alec tried to rise from the over-stuffed couch only to find himself sinking back down.

Grunting, he said, "Give me a hand, will you? This bloody sofa is like quick sand!"

Giggling, she helped him to his feet.

At the Riviera Pool, Alec ordered non-alcoholic drinks, while Michelle chose a table. On his return, he saw that she was sitting in the shade and remarked, "You don't care for the sun, do you?"

She took the glass from his hand and replied, "I like it, but it doesn't like me. Every time I try to get some color, I break out in a rash. I even tried Gwen's suntan oil, but it didn't help."

Though Michelle answered one of the questions that had been bothering Alec, it left plenty of others. Did she kill Mark when she learned he was transferring to another ship without her? Did Gwen witness the incident and try to extort money from Michelle. For that theory to work, it would mean that the masseuse had money, and Gwen thought she could get her hands on it.

Casually, Alec asked Michelle about her home and family. As usual, she needed a one-word prompt before launching into a monologue. During the next few minutes, he learned that she was the only child of elderly and doting parents. Michelle explained that her mother and father were civil servants, and her grandparents owned several shares in a diamond mine. Since her coworkers at the spa often teased her about being a "De Beer," Gwen could have jumped to the wrong conclusion about Michelle's circumstances.

When that subjected was exhausted, Alec remarked, "I saw you with the chief of security. Do I hear wedding bells?"

Michelle blushed and smiled shyly. "Do you know he used to frighten me? We served on the Monoceros together. Every time that Ronald and I were together, I could feel him watching me. It really gave me the creeps."

She stopped a moment to take a sip of her soda and moved closer to Alec. In a low voice, she continued. "He was forced to transfer here because I reported him to the captain. Later on, I found out that I looked like Ronald's fiancée, Sabine. He was heart broken when she died from leukemia and felt happier whenever he was near me. Don't you think that's terribly sad and romantic?"

Alec nodded in a dumbfounded way and said, "Please go on."

"A year ago, I transferred to the Pegasus and ran into Ronald again. He kept his distance from me then. When I started to date Mark, I felt safer, you know, and said hi to him a couple of times. We never became friends, but it was less awkward."

Assuming that Michelle's break would end soon, Alec tried to hurry her along. "When did it become romantic?"

Michelle sighed. "He was so sweet to me after Mark died. He told me that he knew how I felt. We went for walks on the deck, and one night he asked me if he could kiss me. Anyway, we've been seeing each other ever since. You were right when you said that Mark's death would make sense one day. I think it was all part of a big plan!"

Alec wasn't sure whether it was a cosmic plan or Bauer's. After listening to Michelle, Alec had doubts about the security officer's motives, but honestly couldn't visualize her killing Mark or Gwen. She seemed so trusting and helpless.

Moments later, Michelle got up to leave. She gave Alec a quick hug and ran back to the spa.

Before eliminating Michelle from his list of suspects, Alec decided it would be a good idea to return to his office and compare Officer Bauer's personal sales receipts with those of Michelle's. If Alec could find proof that they spent money in the same place, at the same, it would give him reason to believe that their relationship had begun earlier.

Alec stepped into the Bull Dog Pub at two o'clock. Since Jeffrey Sheffield wouldn't be coming for another hour, Alec ordered Glenlivet from the waiter and began to review his day thus far.

He went over the finances of Michelle and Bauer, and was disappointed to learn that they *hadn't* run into each other "accidentally on purpose." The only high spot of the afternoon was seeing Regina in the office. Though she was up to her neck in paperwork, Alec invited her to the pub for a wee nip. She not only turned him down, but also called him "a devil incarnate for corrupting the morals of the elderly."

When Alec's whisky arrived, he was surprised and amused to see Regina approaching his booth. After spilling a bottle of liquid paper on her desk, she decided that an afternoon pick-me-up wouldn't impede her progress after all. Over drinks, Alec told Regina about the budding romance between Bauer and Michelle, and his upcoming interview with Jeffrey.

Regina cautioned Alec to watch his step with the plumber. As to Bauer, she didn't feel he was the sort of man to murder two people, but nonetheless thought it would be prudent to have her friend in human resources fax over their individual personnel records. Even though McGill had already looked through their files, Alec agreed it wouldn't hurt to take a peek.

Jeffrey arrived earlier than expected and Alec wondered whether it had any relationship to his guilt or innocence. Once the introductions were made, Regina quickly finished her drink and departed.

While Alec waited for Jeffrey to be served his Guinness, they made small talk. Jeffrey hadn't heard that Scott Harris left the ship with Eric Santos, and Regina was the new Assistant Controller. For some reason, Jeffrey seemed relieved that Scott was no longer on board the Pegasus.

After Jeffrey's drink was served, Alec began to play hardball. As the plumber was wiping beer froth from his mouth, Alec asked, "So, when did your fling with Gwen Llewelyn begin?"

Appearing shocked, he blurted out, "Oh lord, how did you find out?"

As Alec swiveled the whiskey around in his glass, he replied mundanely, "McGill and I heard it from several sources. We just don't know when your affair started and how it ended. Why don't you tell me about it?"

"Well, you knew Gwen," whispered Jeffrey. "She was unbelievable. Half the time I wasn't sure if she was coming onto me."

"Go on," Alec said reassuringly.

"I met her soon after our tour began in October. She reported a blocked toilet. She watched me fix it the whole time and said she liked men who were good with their hands. Gwen was in this silky bathrobe, and I swear, she let it fall open on purpose. I saw everything. Before I knew it, we were doing it on her bed."

"Did she know you were married?"

"I don't know. Afterward, she gave me this weird smile and told me she might want me from time to time. I felt kind of used."

Alec wondered whether many sexually abused children grew up with such self-destructive tendencies. Gwen certainly had her problems. Wishing Jeffrey had shown more restraint, Alec asked, "How many times did you get together?"

Jeffrey sighed and took a long draught of beer. Maybe six or seven times over a two-month period. Then about a week before Christmas, she told me we were finished. To be honest, it was a relief. I was afraid Nora would find out."

"Did Gwen say why?"

"No, not really."

"What do you mean, not really?"

"Well, she said something about being Santa Claus. It didn't make sense."

To Alec, it made perfect sense. Boyd said that Gwen stopped seeing Jeffrey when she received a visit from his wife. Nora probably warned her to leave him alone.

Up to this point, Jeffrey had been telling the truth. From Alec's copy of the plumbing log, he knew that Gwen had reported seven plumbing "problems" during that time period.

Getting to the end of his current line of questions, Alec asked, "What happened the last time she reported a blockage?"

"You mean on the day the controller died?"

"Aye."

"I got to her cabin that afternoon ready to tell her that I wasn't interested. Since her toilet was really stopped up, I didn't say anything."

"Is that when you found out she was pregnant?"

Within an instant Jeffrey's facial expression changed radically. A glistening layer of sweat formed on his forehead and upper lip.

Jeffrey shrieked. "You sod. You've been playing me all along!"

Although a few heads turned in their direction, Alec gazed at Jeffrey and said quietly, "Just tell me what you found in the toilet vacuum system. It wasn't a book of matches, was it?"

"You bloody well know. That stupid bitch flushed down the plastic pregnancy indicator. Even though the damn thing was in two pieces and standing in the water for hours, it showed *positive*."

"Did Gwen say anything?"

"Yeah. The slut said she had no idea who made her pregnant. But, I was in the running!"

CHAPTER 15

▼

"WEDDING BELL BLUES"

Words & Music—Laura Nyro

Friday Evening—3ʳᵈ of February

The evening promised to be highly enjoyable. It was Regina Hill's first formal night on the Pegasus. Douglas and Alec looked suave in their formal white cutaway jackets, and the ladies were equally breathtaking in their apparel. Regina wore a steel blue, silk dress that matched the color of her eyes, and Paige was tantalizing in an off-the-shoulder dark green gown.

After observing his companions take part in the second seating of the Captain's Welcome Reception, Alec was ready to have his own party. With no effort on his part, he convinced the others to come to the Lido Bar for a little get-together.

While Douglas ordered drinks and snacks at the bar for everyone, Alec stuffed his pipe contently. It was just approaching 9:00 P.M. and the lounge was empty. Passengers from the early shift were being entertained in the Starlight Lounge and those from the late seating were at dinner.

Alec was about to take his first puff when the doctor and bartender brought over their beverages and hors d'oeuvres. Douglas quickly seized the unoccupied chair beside Regina when Alec raised his glass.

Clearing his throat in a dignified fashion, Alec proposed a toast, "To old friends and new acquaintances. May you have your hearts desire!"

Douglas assented, "Here, here," while Alec looked at Paige and smiled. He was sure he knew what Douglas wanted.

Over drinks each of them discussed their plans for Saturday. Since the ship would be at sea for the entire day, Paige expected to be busy at the cruise desk. Regina groaned remembering that the inventory of kitchen foodstuffs was long overdue. And the doctor confirmed he'd be in the infirmary all morning and on call the rest of the day.

Since Alec had remained silent during their interchange, Paige inquired, "Pray tell, what are you planning to do?"

Alec let a circle of smoke waft around his head before he replied. "Let's see. Sometime tomorrow, I have to check my e-mail. I've been waiting to hear from McGill. I'd also like to have a chat with Nora. Douglas, what time will she be in?"

"I hope you're not going to upset her," grunted the doctor.

Seeing Douglas agitated, Regina gently patted his knee. "I know you don't like to see your staff distressed, but I agree with Alec. He needs to find out whether Nora knew of her husband's affair and acted upon it."

Douglas smiled at Regina. "You're right of course, my dear." Addressing himself to Alec he continued. "Visiting hours are over at eleven. Why don't you come by then?"

Alec complied gladly. He was thankful that Regina could smooth out the old bird's ruffled feathers. For the rest of the evening, Douglas and the assistant controller amiably discussed their children and grandchildren.

As it approached ten, Alec began to yawn. Paige reminded him that he hadn't gotten much sleep since Gwen was murdered. Deciding it was time to turn in, Alec and Paige excused themselves, and left the senior citizens to each other and the moonlight.

Alec tried to come up with a plan to handle Nora Sheffield on his way to the infirmary. He wasn't sure how much information to divulge. If Nora hadn't heard about Jeffrey's infidelity, Alec didn't want to be the first one to tell her. If she did know, it would put her on the top of Alec's list of suspects.

When he arrived, Nora was in the midst of bandaging a young boy's bruised knee. After the child scampered off with his father, Alec asked for the doctor. Before she could respond, Douglas came out of his inner office with Janet Kane.

"Speak of the devil," said Alec.

Douglas smiled at Janet. "It just so happens we were talking about you too!" cooed the doctor.

Janet lightly touched the doctor's arm to stop him from saying anything more. She then turned her attention to Alec, and said, "I was hoping we could talk privately."

Alec grinned. "I'd be delighted. When and where?"

"I was planning to cool off in the Lido pool and then have a bite to eat. When you're finished here, please come join me."

As she walked out of the room all eyes followed her. Under his breath, Alec muttered, "God, she's bewitching!"

A moment later the spell was broken. Alec remembered he had job to do and casually said to Nora, "If you're not too busy now, I'd like to speak to you."

Nora nodded and sighed, as if she had the weight of the world on her shoulders. Alec assumed she knew what was coming and felt somewhat relieved. They took seats in the doctor's recently vacated office. Alec could smell Janet's exotic perfume and hoped he would be able to concentrate.

Before Alec could say anything, Nora declared angrily, "Jeffrey told me what happened yesterday. You had some nerve to treat him like a criminal!"

Alec was a bit stunned by her reaction, but understood that Nora was between a proverbial rock and a hard place. She had to stand by him or leave him. She appeared to choose the former, at least, for the time being.

When she seemed a bit calmer, Alec said, "You've known a long time, haven't you, that Jeffrey was seeing Gwen?"

"No, I just found out!"

"Nora, don't bother lying to me. Boyd told me that you visited Gwen a week before Christmas."

"It's not t…" gasped Nora. Her posture changed abruptly and her face contorted in pain. "I hate him. I hate him! He promised to keep his hands to himself."

Alec wasn't prepared for her next move. She threw her arms around him and started to sob violently against his chest. Startled, Alec murmured reassurances, thinking all the time, "I'd make a bloody useless homicide detective. McGill would be laughing his head off."

Finally her tears subsided, and Alec was able to extricate himself from her embrace to go in search of tissues.

When he stepped into the waiting area, Douglas glared at him. "I heard her cry. Did you have to be so rough?"

Alec would have gotten angry, if it hadn't been so ridiculous. He replied, "I haven't even started yet," as he took a box of Kleenex from the counter and a bottle of water from the infirmary refrigerator.

On returning, Nora appeared to be more composed. Alec put the items on the doctor's desk while she apologized. "I'm sorry for carrying on. It's not your fault, he's such a louse."

Not wanting to cause any more hysterics, Alec asked gently, "When did you find out about Jeffrey and Gwen?"

Wiping her nose, she responded, "I've always been suspicious of Gwen. Even though she flirted with everyone, she acted especially friendly toward Jeffrey.

"Just before the holidays, I overheard him talking to Patrick, the plumber from Dublin. Pat asked Jeffrey why he kept repairing the toilet in Cabin 867. When I realized it was Gwen's room, I put two and two together."

"How did Gwen react when you confronted her?"

"It was strange. She acted like a little girl who had been caught pulling the cat's tail. She said she was very sorry and wouldn't do it again."

Gazing at Alec with an expression of uncertainty, Nora added, "I think I'd better tell you the whole story. Days before I spoke to Gwen, I found out I was pregnant. I told her hoping she'd leave Jeffrey alone. Looking back, I don't think it was really necessary. She seemed to have her sights set on someone else."

While Alec tried to envision who that was and how far along Gwen had been in her own pregnancy, Nora continued. "I haven't told anyone that I'm expecting. I wanted to complete my first trimester before telling Jeffrey and Dr. Abbot. It's at the end of *this* month!"

Alec congratulated her and prayed that Jeffrey would keep his pants on in the future. He also began to doubt that Nora had a good reason to poison Gwen. Jeffrey's affair had ended with Gwen long before she died, and Nora had no motive to kill Mark Linley. Alec decided it would be best to avoid the subject of Gwen's pregnancy for the time being. Besides, all the ands, ifs, and buts, were giving Alec a royal headache.

Before going their separate ways, Nora thanked Alec for being so understanding. She gave him a peck on the cheek and said, "I wish Jeffrey were more like you. Paige is very lucky."

Although Alec was eager to see Janet next, he stopped off at his cabin first. His white uniform was smudged with black mascara, and he wanted to change into a bathing suit just in case Ms. Kane wanted to converse in the hot tub.

Alec had no trouble spotting Janet on the Lido Deck. Several men were gathered around her in the fresh water pool. Sighting Alec, she called, "I'll be right out. Take the lounge chair next to mine. It's the one with Rex Stout book on it."

Alec raised his voice over the steel drum band that was performing and shouted, "I'm going to the bar for a cold drink. What can I get you?"

"A bloody Mary would be nice, with two sticks of celery."

Alec was in the mood for something refreshing, so he decided to try the ship's drink for the day—a virgin Bahamas Mama. When he returned with the glasses, Janet was stretched out on the deck chair.

Standing over her, Alec noticed her petite and nicely proportioned figure. She was provocatively dressed in a strapless one-piece bathing suit. Her well-defined upper arm muscles were the only part of her body that detracted from her appearance.

As Alec set down the drinks on a small snack table, Janet cleared away her belonging from his chair. "I know I'm not supposed to save seats, but I felt a bit wicked this morning."

Alec observed the opened book at her feet, and said, "I've read almost every Nero Wolfe novel. I really like mysteries in which all the suspects are assembled in one room and the killer is about to me named. They're so neat and cozy."

"Speaking of murder," Janet remarked with a lively expression, "I wanted to talk to you about my fiancé Rick. Do you really believe he was involved in the ghastly deaths of both the controller and Gwen?"

Answering a question with a question, Alec said, "Did you want to say something on his behalf? He hasn't been very forthcoming with me or the sheriff."

While Janet sipped her Bloody Mary, Alec could see that she was choosing her next words carefully. After she placed her glass back on the table, she confided, "When I joined the cruise Wednesday, I found out that Rick was quite angry with you. Though he doesn't know that I'm speaking to you now, I thought it would be a good idea to clear the air."

Uncertain of what she knew, Alec said, "I think that's very wise. Can you tell me about Rick's relationships with Mark Linley and Gwen Llewelyn?"

Alec sounded calm when he uttered those words, but he felt terribly excited. He hoped to hear some small detail that would implicate Rick in the murders.

Janet began earnestly. "I know for a fact that my fiancé saw very little of Mark, and he neither liked or disliked him. Rick told me that his department always exceeded its goals for bingo. He had no motive to kill that poor man.

"Gwen was another matter," she continued. "When Rick and I met, he told me that he wasn't seeing anyone on the ship. A few months later, I learned that he and Gwen were involved. I was upset when I found out he was dating *her* while he was also seeing me, but I forgave him. After all, he's a very desirable man, and I know that whore made it difficult for him to end their fling."

The "whore" remark stung Alec like a slap on the cheek. Up until then, Janet's remarks had been guarded and circumspect. Now she appeared bitter and driven to get married, regardless of the outcome.

Her attitude reminded Alec of the words in "Wedding Bell Blues." Laura Nyro wrote, "I was the one who came runnin' when you were lonely, I haven't lived one day not lovin' you only." The double negative in the lyrics made Alec wonder about Janet's motives. Did she kill Gwen to remove her competition? Although Alec felt that Janet was capable of murder, she had no logical reason to want Mark dead.

When they finished their drinks, Alec suggested lunch. He had begun to feel uncomfortable in the hot sun and hoped that different surroundings would encourage her to reveal more.

Over a pleasant meal in the Lido Restaurant, Alec found out about her past. Douglas had surmised correctly. She had been married to the prominent plastic surgeon. She glossed over the seamy details of her divorce, but mentioned that she had received a handsome settlement that enabled her to buy a travel agency in Boca Raton.

Janet saw Rick as a complement to herself. His family was renown in the community, and she "adored" going to Greenwood Hunt Club functions with Rick's parents when he was unable to attend.

Though Alec wanted to keep her talking, he couldn't help reacting to her reference to the *hunt club*. Surprised, Alec exclaimed, "What? They hunt foxes in the States?"

Janet tried to conceal her amusement as she replied, "No, not anymore. The club was founded in 1879 for the local gentry. Today it's considered very exclusive and 'old money.' It's one of the few private clubs in America that has grass tennis courts, not to mention a fabulous golf course. Rick's parents have sponsored us for membership. It's a dream come true for me."

It seemed to Alec that they were perfectly suited to each other. She wanted to be connected to a prestigious family and he needed a limitless supply of cash. Although Ms. Kane admitted to "putting away some money," Alec couldn't imagine that her savings, no matter how large, were enough to keep up with Rick's gambling habit.

At 1: 30, Janet left Alec's side. She was eager to get out of her wet bathing suit and attend a body-conditioning seminar at the spa. Alec had discovered quite a bit about Janet, but remained curious as to why she craved notoriety.

Later that afternoon, Alec stopped by the Dolphin Room to check his electronic mail. As he approached the lounge, he heard the sound of cheering coming from the television set. Milos Radovanovic was its only occupant. Alec hadn't seen him since the day that they lunched together. Milos was literally on the edge of his seat, eating a hero sandwich and watching a sportscast. Trying not to disturb him, Alec mumbled hello and parked himself at the computer.

It didn't take long for Alec to log on and print out the message he was expecting from McGill. Before Alec could give it more than a cursory glance, Milos turned off the TV set and walked over to him.

"You must think I'm terribly rude. I wanted to catch a basketball score." Ready for conversation, he asked, "How's your investigation going?"

Alec grinned at the young man, remembering what it was like to lose himself in a sporting event. As he brought his attention back to the present, Alec thoughtfully replied, "This case is like a giant jigsaw puzzle. I think I have all the pieces, but I'm still missing the big picture."

"Is there anything I can do?"

Recalling how much Milos had known about Coral Cay, Alec asked, "What do you know about Martinique? I plan to go ashore tomorrow and visit some of the drug stores in town."

Milos laughed. "You didn't hear? I'm now the port and shopping specialist on board. Santos didn't give Captain Jarvis any notice when he left with Scott Harris. They replaced him with yours truly. I'll be giving a talk in the Starlight Lounge shortly. Why don't you tag along?"

"That would be great," grinned Alec as he shoved the unread e-mail into his pocket. On the way to the "lecture hall," they stopped off at the front office long enough to pick up a box of leaflets and maps.

Unlike the last time he was present at a discussion of the ports, Alec watched from the front of the lounge and paid strict attention. He learned that Martinique was a department and region of France, represented in the French Parliament. Since the ship was going to be docked in Fort-de-France, Milos told Alec to frequent the businesses along the rues Schoelcher, Victor Hugo, and Antoine Siger.

Alec returned to his cabin with a map of the shopping district that identified the major stores and streets in the vicinity. Milos didn't know whether nicotine patches were sold in *les pharmacies*, but Alec felt certain he'd enjoy finding out on his own.

Before making another move, however, Alec dug out McGill's e-mail. Sitting on the corner of his bed, he read:

Subj: Investigation of Gwen Llewelyn
Date: 4th February, 9:17:01 AM EST
From: Dan.McGill@coflso.net
To: AlecDunBarton@aol.com

Sorry it took so long to contact you. After thoroughly examining the credit card transactions of the suspects, we were disappointed to learn that *no one* purchased nicotine patches. Since the perpetrator probably bought the product in your neck of the woods or used cash, our field is limited. We plan to canvas neighborhood drug stores of those crewmembers who reside in Florida. I hope you have better luck on your end.

The crime scene unit found nothing of consequence in the victim's room. The plumber's fingerprints were located near the toilet, and Tanner's were discovered on a bathroom shelf. Griffin's prints were prominent throughout the cabin. After testing all of Gwen's cosmetics and drug items, the forensics unit didn't find any other poisonous substances.

The preliminary autopsy was correct. Llewelyn was three month's pregnant, and her toxicology screen revealed that she was topically poisoned by a lethal dose of nicotine. Further tests of the adhesive in the suntan oil may point us to the brand name and/or its country of origin.

As to the father of Gwen's baby, it was Boyd Griffin.

I wish I had more to tell you. If we don't crack this case soon, it may never get solved. We have plenty of suspects and not a shred of evidence.

Please keep me informed.

Dan McGill

Although, McGill's news sounded bleak, Alec thought about the conversation he just had with Milos. He was quite sure that the pieces to the puzzle would fit together soon.

CHAPTER 16

▼

"She's Not There"

Words & Music—Rod Argent

Saturday Evening—4th of February

During dinner, Alec told Paige and Regina about his plans to go into Fort-de-France the following day and asked whether either of them could join him. Regina sadly shook her head and said she still had too much paperwork.

Paige, on the other hand, was ready for a day away from the Pegasus. She spoke French fluently and wanted to make sure that Alec didn't misbehave. Although England and France had been allies for well over a century, Paige remarked to Regina that several of the English crewmembers still had a regrettable habit of calling their French neighbors "froggies." She expected they in turn, called the Brits "limies."

When Paige finished her meal, she briefly explained that she couldn't stay for coffee. She needed to meet with several couples to discuss FCL's Adriatic Coast Cruise. As Alec handed her the cabin key he obtained for her the other day, she whispered in his ear, "I'll see you later. Don't have too much fun without me!"

With a tender expression, he watched her walk toward the elevators. Regina couldn't help noticing his demeanor.

"Does she know that you love her?"

"What do you mean?" responded Alec a bit too vehemently.

Regina searched Alec's face for a moment before replying. "Alec, I haven't known you long, but I can see that there's something in your past preventing you from embracing your future. You live day by day. You never talk about your family or your life in the U.K. What happened?"

Wishing his lemonade were a Scotch, Alec told her about his wife and daughter.

When he finished, Regina said, "I now understand what's holding you back. But one of these days, you're going to have to make an emotional commitment to living again."

Alec knew she was right. There had been many times during the week that he wanted to tell Paige how he felt. Although it was very easy to make *love* to her, Alec was reluctant to say what was in his heart. He felt that those three little words would mark the end of their relationship. He only lost people he loved.

After several moments, Alec smiled wanly. "Don't worry about me. Once this murder investigation is over, I'll be forced to face my fears and decide whether to return to London."

Regina nodded, and changed the subject by asking, "So what's on the agenda tonight?"

With a sparkle in his eyes, he said, "We're going on a treasure hunt. If you help me find what I need, I may just buy you a drink!"

In the Constellation Lounge, Alec and Regina savored their well-earned Scotches. They had traipsed from the Photo Gallery to the photography lab and then on to the publication center. Regina met Alfie, the young lad who had wanted to sell photos of Mark Linley's dead body to the tabloids. After it was all said and done, Alec found what he needed—pictures of all his suspects. He and Paige would not be going into Martinique empty handed.

It had been simple for him to acquire a portrait of Janet Kane from the gallery shop. Photographers throughout the ship spent their day taking snapshots of passengers dining, dancing, and relaxing. Since Flagship Cruise line proudly displayed photos of its officers along the walls of the corridors, Alec was able to get a print of Bauer. Alfie also had group shots of spa employees and infirmary staff. Locating a picture of the plumber posed the biggest problem. Alec was finally able to find one of Jeffrey Sheffield in an archive file at the printing center.

While Regina was flexing her sore ankles, she said, "We certainly hit the mother lode. What are you planning to do with them?"

Alec grinned. "You know, I'm not really sure. Now that I have photos of this motley crew, Paige and I can show them to the local pharmacists in town. Gwen's killer would have needed to purchase three boxes of nicotine patches to poison the entire eight ounce bottle of suntan oil. I hope one of my suspects will be recognized. It may be a waste of time, but worth a try."

As Alec sorted through his mug shots, he heard a voice behind him. "Are you starting a fan club?" asked Douglas.

"It's more likely that one of these people is a *fan*atic. Of what, I'm not certain,"

"May I see them?"

Alec handed the photographs to the doctor. Douglas sifted through them and paused at the one of himself with Beth, Nora, and Maggie. Sounding slightly vexed, he said, "You not including me in your list of suspects, are you?"

In response, Alec quipped, "Would you like me to blacken out your features with a magic marker?"

Although Douglas laughed it off, Alec wondered what alarmed his good friend. Was he concerned that someone on the island would identify him? Did the doctor kill Mark for some heinous offense and poison Gwen to shut her up?

Feeling troubled by these questions, Alec decided to retreat to his cabin. He would rest much easier once the killer was caught and brought to justice.

Alec entered his cabin and heard the water running in the shower. When he peaked into the bathroom, he saw Paige partly covered by the shower curtain and soap bubbles. Donning his clothes in five seconds flat, Alec stepped into the tub. Paige cried, "Oh Alec, what are you do...ing." It then became very quiet, except for an occasional ooh and ah.

At 7:00 A.M., the ship docked in Martinique. Alec had wanted to get an early start, but he and Paige weren't able to disembark until well after eight. Despite the lateness, there were still a large number of tour busses waiting to take passengers from the ship to their excursion sites.

Since Alec and Paige knew they'd be doing plenty of walking once they arrived at the city center, they hired a taxicab for nine dollars. During the short drive, Paige pointed out various landmarks and restaurants. She remarked that the town was a cross between the French Riviera and New Orleans.

Although some parts of town appeared shabbier than others, Alec found the colorful shops and bargain-hungry shoppers mesmerizing. So much was happening in a small vicinity. Alec realized that the Pegasus was like a sterile lab in comparison.

Over a two-hour period, Alec and Paige visited six drug stores that sold nicotine inhalers and gums. Alec was pleased that these non-smoking aids could be purchased in Martinique without a prescription, but disappointed he hadn't found a pharmacy that sold nicotine patches. Tired and irritable, they decided that lunch would boost their sagging morale.

Knowing that Alec's taste in food ran to the traditional, Paige suggested a cozy café that offered French fare as opposed to spicy Creole cuisine. Even though their feet had begun to ache, they continued on to Rue Ernest Deproge for lunch. After enjoying a sumptuous meal of shredded cocoanut salad, Caribbean red snapper, and several dessert crepes, Alec found what he had been seeking.

Opposite the restaurant was a small well-stocked drug store. Displayed in its window were boxes of *Nicotinell*, the French version of the nicotine patch. The cartons contained medication for seven and twenty-eight days, and the doses ranged from seven to twenty-one milligrams. Optimistic that Gwen's murderer obtained the patches from this store, Alec rushed into the pharmacy ahead of Paige.

Alec targeted a woman in a lab coat and spoke to her in a torrent of English. While Paige removed the oversized photos from her tote bag, she interrupted him, "Let me speak to her. When you're aroused, your Scottish accent becomes more marked."

Thankful for her assistance, Alec stepped back from the register and watched Paige as she took over in French. Alec could only follow a few words here and there. After what seemed like an interminable time, the sales woman took the pictures from Paige's outstretched hand. She glimpsed at them and exclaimed, "*C'est l'homme tres blanc du bateau.*"

Alec understood that *homme* meant man. Trying to recall what *blanc* meant, he thought of a dessert he liked—*blancmange,* a white custard made with milk, sugar, and cornstarch. The only "white man" that came to mind was Bauer. Barely containing his excitement, Alec gently nudged Paige in the ribcage. "Ask her what he purchased and when."

While Alec watched the animated expressions on the pharmacist's face, Paige translated fragments of their conversation.

"She definitely recognizes Ronald Bauer.

"He bought one box of Nicotinell.

"About three weeks ago.

"He wanted a 28-day supply.

"Of the highest dosage—21 milligrams.

"He used cash."

Alec was thrilled with the information. After thanking the clerk, Alec and Paige headed back to the Pegasus. Alec knew that the discovery didn't prove that Bauer killed Gwen Llewelyn. The security chief purchased only twenty-eight patches. Gwen's suntan oil had contained nearly three times that amount. Of course, it didn't rule him out either. It was possible that Bauer obtained patches from other drug stores along the ship's route.

Once back on board, Alec sought out Bauer. From one of the security staff, Alec learned that Bauer was investigating the disappearance of some jewelry from a passenger's cabin and would be tied up most of the day. Deciding to speak to him at another time, Alec revised his plans.

Moments later Alec knocked on Boyd's cabin door, half hoping there'd be no response. Boyd answered right away and said, "I was wondering when I'd be hearing from you. You're here about the paternity test, aren't you?"

"Yes laddy, I found out yesterday. Can I have a word with you now?"

Boyd waved him in and offered him a warm bottle of soda.

Alec refused, took a chair next to the table, and glanced around the room. Boyd had tried to make the cabin look less like its cookie cutter twins with portraits of some of the great jazz musicians. There was John Coltrane, Miles Davis, Thelonious Monk, and Stan Getz.

Standing rigidly by his bed, Boyd asked. "Well, what did McGill say? Was I the father of Gwen's baby?"

Answering his question directly, Alec said, "Yes Laddy, you were."

On hearing the news Boyd's posture crumbled. He sat down warily and asked, "Are they sure?"

Alec nodded. Since he could add nothing to his last statement, Alec waited for Boyd to say something. After a few seconds, Alec broke the uncomfortable silence and asked, "So, what are your plans? Are you still going to take the job in New York?"

Sounding more resolute, Boyd replied. "This is my last cruise. When the ship docks this Friday, I'll meet with McGill, and then take the next plane to Toronto. After I see my folks, I'm going to pick up my car and drive to New York City. I've had enough of this place. She's gone and no one can bring her back."

The chorus of to "She's Not There" came to Alec's mind. The Zombies sang, "Well let me tell you 'bout the way she looked, The way she acted, and the colour of her hair, Her voice was soft and cool, her eyes were clear and bright. But she's not there."

Alec understood his pain all too well. Boyd needed to get away from everything and everyone that reminded him of Gwen. Although running from the past sounded like a good solution, Alec thought about the advice Regina gave him just the other night.

His attention was brought back to the present as Boyd asked, "Do you have any idea who murdered her?"

Alec didn't want to give Boyd false hope and said, "No," all the time trusting that his Scottish "canny" instincts wouldn't let him down.

Shortly afterward, Alec left. He wanted a cold beverage and a hot shower in that order. On the way to the restaurant, Alec thought about his next move.

That evening, Alec and Paige sat on "their couch" in the Lido Bar. Alec puffed on pipe and blew smoke rings, trying to put the case into perspective.

Paige remarked, "You look preoccupied. Would it help if we made some notes? I can get a pen and pad from the beauty spa."

"You'll be my gal Friday?"

"Of course," she replied. Paige shoved he tired feet in her shoes and started to walk to the other side of the Lido Deck.

Paige soon returned carrying a pile of papers and a clipboard, "I found these medical questionnaires. The reverse side is completely blank. Do you think they will do?"

Grinning, Alec replied, "I'm sure they're fine. We'll start by listing the suspects. Below each name we can then specify whether they had motive and opportunity."

Alec rattled off the names of Jeffrey and Nora Sheffield, Michelle Van Dam, Ronald Bauer, Rick Tanner, Janet Kane, and Boyd Griffin. Stopping for a moment, he asked, "Did I miss anyone?"

Paige chewed on the end of her pen thoughtfully. "You once thought that Gwen could have killed Mark. Have you changed your mind?"

"No, you better put her on the bottom of the list along with Scott Harris and Eric Santos. I really don't think they were involved, but you never know."

When they completed the first project, Alec instructed Paige to begin another list containing information about the two murder weapons. Under the headings "dumbbell" and "nicotine," she recorded the names of the suspects who had access to and knowledge of those particular instruments of death.

For their final task, they constructed a timeline. Alec and Paige started with the Gwen's relationship with Jeffrey Sheffield at the end of October and brought it forward to the present. In between, they noted Rick's engagement to Janet, Rick's breakup with Gwen, Nora's pregnancy and confrontation with Gwen, Scott's theft of the champagne, Bauer's purchase of nicotine patches, Mark's last supper, Gwen's pregnancy test, Mark's bludgeoning, Gwen's engagement and death, and Michelle's new beau.

Once they finished, Paige looked at Alec and softly asked, "Did you find any of this beneficial?"

Alec laughed heartily. "This timeline hasn't helped me figure out who killed Mark Linley and Gwen Llewelyn, but I can show you at what point I got my headache!"

CHAPTER 17

▼

"WHITE RABBIT"

Words & Music—Grace Slick

Monday Morning—6ᵗʰ of February

Alec had several hours to kill before the ship docked in Barbados at 11:00 A.M. Eager to make good use of that time, Alec called Bauer to see whether they could meet. Although the security officer had breakfasted earlier, he agreed to join Alec in the Lido Restaurant.

When Bauer arrived, Alec was already seated at a corner table for two, adding cream and sugar to his bowl of oatmeal. While Bauer made his way to the beverage bar for a cup of tea, Alec tasted the cereal and winced in dismay, wondering what was wrong with it. On returning, the chief of security saw Alec's pained expression and practically screamed, "My God, has someone else died?"

Confused, Alec glanced at Bauer. "No. Why would you say that?"

"You seemed really disturbed! What happened?"

Alec grinned. "I guess I did look strange. But this porridge has no flavor or texture. It tastes like wallpaper paste."

"I suspect you're used to steel-cut oats in Scotland," murmured Bauer.

Alec quickly decided it was inedible and excused himself to look for something more appetizing. Moments later, he reappeared with fried eggs and bacon. As Alec was dipping a piece of buttered toast in his yolk, he said, "I wanted to speak to you yesterday, but I heard you had trouble with a crewmember."

Bauer sipped his tea and remarked, "I was tied up for half the day. One of the cabin stewards was accused of stealing a diamond ring and bracelet from a passenger's cabin. When my team searched the fellow's things, they found those items, as well as a man's watch, concealed under his mattress. Afterward he became violent, and my men were forced to lock him up in the ship's brig."

"What are you going to do with him?"

"We'll keep him behind bars until we dock in Fort Lauderdale. If the passenger wants to press charges, the police can have him. If not, he'll be sent back to his country."

Deciding it was the right time to bring up Gwen's death, Alec remarked, "By the way, I heard from McGill. Gwen *was* topically poisoned. It appears that the killer used nicotine patches to taint her suntan oil."

On hearing the news, Bauer gasped and exclaimed, "I had a box of that vile stuff!"

Still stunned, he explained, "I decided to quit smoking a few weeks ago and bought a pack of nicotine patches in Martinique. Not long after trying them, I began to experience dizziness and nausea. At first, I thought it was the stomach flu. But later, I found out that I should have been on seven milligrams and *not* twenty-one."

As Alec listened, several questions came to mind. Voicing one, he asked, "Who told you that you were on the wrong dosage?"

"It was Rick Tanner. He tried the patch last year."

"How did the topic come up?"

"I ran into him at the duty-free shop while I was buying cigarettes. I told Rick that I tried Nicotinell and it made me ill."

Alec made a mental note to add that incident to the timeline that he and Paige constructed last night. After swallowing the rest of his lukewarm coffee in one gulp, he continued, "What did you do with the rest of the patches? You must have had a large supply left."

Bauer nodded. "I put them on a shelf in my bathroom. The plumber who fixed my faucet said he wanted to stop smoking, so I gave him the box. I told him to read the pamphlet that came with it. The instructions were written in French and English. That was about two weeks ago. Do you think he poisoned Gwen?"

Not ready to get into it, Alec asked, "Which plumber was it? Patrick or Jeffrey?"

"Oh, the English one."

Certain that Patrick was from Ireland, a sense of good will pervaded Alec. He had finally begun to amass some circumstantial evidence. After doing a bit more digging in Bridgetown and Philipsburg, Alec thought he'd be able to unmask the murderer.

Anxious to set off on his quest, Alec got up from the table and warmly grasped Bauer's hand in thanks. The security chief seemed surprised by Alec's sudden display of affection, but continued to sip his tea thoughtfully.

Before Alec could disembark for Barbados, he stopped off at his stateroom to pick up the photos of his suspects. Unsure where Paige left them, he began to nose around and found them in her tote bag, leaning against the dresser. As Alec yanked the large envelope from her canvas bag, Paige's suntan oil dropped out. It was Cruisin' Coconut, the brand Gwen used.

While Alec stared at the bottle on the floor, he experienced a terrible sense of anxiety. He knew Paige was innocent, but the ghosts in *his* past continued to haunt him. Hating his reaction, Alec examined his emotions.

His fears stemmed from his inability to direct his future. He couldn't save his family or take comfort in knowing his life would unfold as he'd planned. As he replaced the suntan oil in Paige's tote, Alec made a vow to himself to let go and let God take over. He was so sick and tired of trying to control everything.

Feeling somewhat better, Alec started to walk to the debarkation area. Along the way, the captain announced on the loudspeaker that the local authorities cleared the ship and guests could proceed ashore.

Although several vessels were docked at the port, Alec was able to reach the air-conditioned passenger terminal easily. The large facility not only housed a post office, a tourist bureau, and an excursion desk, but also a multiple of duty-free shops and pushcart vendors selling luxury goods and Barbadian crafts.

Determined not to wander all over Bridgetown in search of drug stores, Alec entered the tourist center. The agent was extremely helpful and gave him a photocopied list of pharmacies from the Barbados Yellow Pages. She explained that most of the drug stores were on High, Broad, and Lower Broad Streets. Equipped with a map, Alec was ready to visit Bridgetown.

Since the downtown area was about a mile away from the cruise-ship terminal, Alec took a two-dollar van ride to the first drug store. He felt quite at home being driven on the left side of the road. He was doubly glad to have taken the taxi when he grasped how long and dusty the walk would have been.

Over the next few hours, Alec went pharmacy hopping. The stores in Barbados, like their French counterpart, sold nicotine patches without prescriptions. What surprised Alec was the disparity in dosages. French and American patches contained 7, 14, and 21 milligrams of nicotine, while the ones sold in Barbados were in increments of 5, 10, and 15 milligrams. Since none of Alec suspects had been seen purchasing the non-smoking aid, Alec turned his attention to other matters.

He decided to return to Sterlings, a large department store he passed earlier on Broad Street. En route, Alec stopped off at a Chefette, a Barbadian fast food restaurant that offered barbequed chicken, steak, and hamburgers. Convinced he was about to faint from the lack of food, Alec ordered a double-decker burger special and a thick shake. It came to 15.95 BD dollars, which was equivalent to about 8.00 US dollars.

By the time Alec arrived at the store, he was in the mood to shop. First on his agenda was to buy Paige a present. He walked over to one of the fine jewelry counters and was astounded by the choice. After a short wait, a salesperson came to his aid and helped him pick out a heart-shaped gold locket. While she wrapped it up, Alec spotted Janet Kane approaching him with several large shopping bags.

As she began to pass him, Alec tapped her lightly on the shoulder. "Where are you going?"

Fiercely, she turned around and hissed. "If you touch me again, I'll call a cop." When she saw it was Alec, she smiled apologetically. "You scared me half to death."

"Let me make it up to you. Give me a few of your things."

Before Alec could take her parcels, a voice behind him called, "Sir, don't forget your merchandise!"

Slightly abashed, Alec took the package, and graciously thanked the clerk. Turning his attention back to Janet, he asked, "Are you finished shopping or do you have other stops to make?"

"No, I'm done. Am I keeping you from anything?"

Alec would have liked to see the rest of the store. It reminded him of Marks and Spencers. Not wanting her to feel uncomfortable, he answered, "I have what I came for."

"Is it a present for Paige?" teased Janet. "Rick told me that you're like two peas in a pod."

Even though he didn't answer, Alec felt sure that Janet knew the answer from his expression.

In front of National Heroes Square, they caught a cab to the dock. In the taxi, Janet told Alec that she had just listed her name on the bridal registry at the department store. Alec hoped she wasn't fishing for a wedding gift from him. Noticing that she had a number of shopping bags for someone who was about to get married in two and a half months, he asked, "What in the world did you buy today?"

Janet laughed. "I bought bridal favors for Rick's best man, my maid of honor, and two of our friends. I also purchased a set of stainless steel Sheffield knives. I didn't register for them since it's bad luck to receive them for a wedding present."

Hearing "Sheffield" mentioned, Alec's thoughts turned to Jeffrey. He decided to hold off questioning him about the nicotine patches until he visited the pharmacies in St. Maarten.

For the rest of the afternoon, Alec planned to take it easy. Paige was anxious to attend the Flower-Power Party in the Constellation Lounge at seven thirty. Partial to the music from the late 1960's, Alec didn't need much convincing.

When they returned to the ship, Alec escorted Janet to her stateroom. She had a small inside cabin on the Marine Deck. Alec thought it sensible for her to take one of the cheapest lodgings on the Pegasus since she spent most of her time with Rick.

Although Janet invited him in, Alec turned her down. He was exhausted from the heat and wanted to take a "wee" nap before dinner.

"Wake up! You're going to sleep the whole night away."

Alec grinned wondering how long Paige tried to rouse him. He knew he slept like the dead. Alec glanced at the alarm clock and was surprised to see that it was already six thirty. As he sat up, he saw that Paige had an impish expression on her face.

Amused, he demanded, "What's going on here? Do you have something behind your back?"

Paige pulled out a tie-dyed tee shirt and dress. Like a child home from an arts and crafts class, she proudly exclaimed, "Look what I made!"

Amused, Alec replied, "Is that for tonight's festivities?"

"Mmm, yes. Isn't it just perfect? Faith, the assistant cruise director, helped me color the material. We're going to make 'far out' hippies."

"I happened to get you a gift also."

Alec took the small box from the end table and handed it to her. Paige sat on the edge of the bed with an air of expectancy. She squealed in delight as she lifted the cover and gently removed the locket from its velvet-lined container. In an awed tone, she cried, "It's so beautiful, Alec. What's the occasion? My birthday isn't until April."

Hoarsely, Alec replied, "I've been a bit lax in showing you how I feel." Though, the words were on the tip of his tongue, Alec couldn't bring himself to say, "I love you." Unable to make that commitment, he reverted back to his old ways. Alec moved his lips to hers and kissed her with a passion that was intermingled with devotion.

Alec and Paige arrived at the Flower-Power Party fashionably late. Faith was stationed at the door handing out daisies, bandannas, and colorful necklaces. Many of the passengers were dressed in outfits that were suggestive of the 1960's. Alec felt as though he had just stepped back in time. Appropriately, the disc jockey played "The Age of Aquarius" from the musical *Hair*.

Finding a free table proved to be difficult. A young couple eventually waved them over and told them that they were leaving to make the second dinner seating. Alec and Paige gratefully slipped into their seats after they departed.

With Paige guarding their spot, Alec ordered drinks from the bar and rounded up some munchies. The snacks complemented the party's theme and consisted of chips and dip, natural trail mix, vegetable and fruit platters, sunflower seed cookies, and "Alice B. Toklas" brownies. Once they were settled, Alec raised his voice over the din, and asked, "How are you doing?"

He thought Paige looked adorable in her tie-dyed outfit. The neckline of Empire-styled dress accentuated her breasts and showed off the locket perfectly.

She smiled at Alec's approving stare. "I'm fine. I just wish it was less noisy and crowded."

Recognizing that conversation was going to be difficult, Alec sat back and listened to the music. The DJ spun songs by The Doors, Janis Joplin, Jimmy Hendrix, and Cream. During slower selections by The Association, The Mammas and the Papas, Donovan, and Richie Havens, Alec danced with Paige. It wasn't until the song "White Rabbit," was played that Alec had an epiphany of sorts.

It began innocently enough. Since his feet were tired from keeping in step with the music, Alec started to sing out loud. "One pill makes you larger, And one pill makes you small."

Throughout the song, Grace Slick refers to the drug culture and Carroll's *Alice's Adventures in Wonderland*. As he sang, "When logic and proportion, Have fallen sloppy dead, And the White Knight is talking backwards," the hair on Alec's neck stood on end.

Not sure of its significance, Alec compared the lyrics of the song to the murder case. It was true that his mind was moving slow and that logic was failing him. But, it wasn't until Alec got to the word "backwards" that he shouted to Paige. "It's *backwards*! The whole bloody thing is backwards."

"What's backward?"

"The murders. They're backward."

"What do you mean?"

Unable to sit still, Alec rushed to the bar to grab a paper napkin and a pen. When he returned, he began to draw a timeline similar to the one he and Paige constructed last night—but with one very big difference. As he handed her the napkin, his eyes took on an eerie glint.

Paige studied the diagram for a while trying to decipher Alec's handwriting. When she finally understood his scribble, she asked, "Why did you place Gwen's murder *before* Mark's?"

"Because, she was dead the moment she started to carry around the poisoned suntan oil."

"Do you know who killed Gwen and Mark then?"

With a Mona Lisa smile, Alec replied. "Yes. I believe I do."

CHAPTER 18

▼

"THIS IS IT"

Words & Music—Kenny Loggins & Michael McDonald

Tuesday Morning—7th of February

Alec awoke to the robust smell of freshly brewed coffee. Realizing that he'd fallen asleep on the couch in the officer's lounge, Alec opened his eyes expeditiously and discovered Widarta bending over him.

"Would you like some coffee Mr. Alec? It just finished dripping."

Alec grunted in the affirmative and moved his body to an upright position.

"You like it with cream and no sugar. Right?"

"Yes. That would be lovely."

Gratefully, Alec took the cup from Widi.

While he drank down the hot liquid, Alec reviewed the previous evening. After he and Paige returned from the party, Alec found it impossible to sleep. He left Paige to slumber peacefully, and he withdrew to the Dolphin Room, hoping to arrange his chaotic thoughts. Up until he dozed off on the couch, Alec theorized that one particular woman ruthlessly killed two people.

Widarta gazed at Alec like a mother about to scold her errant child. "Did you have a fight with Miss Paige?" he snapped.

Just as Alec was about to reply, Paige rushed in. "Oh here you are. When I woke up and saw you were gone, I began to worry."

Alec grinned at Paige and Widi. "Can't an old Scottish gentleman fall asleep on the settee without everyone falling into a tizzy?"

While Paige refilled Alec's coffee cup and one for herself, Alec warmed to the knowledge that he had found a home aboard the Pegasus. Alec knew that he'd soon have to make a decision about his own future if the killer was whom he suspected.

After Widarta left the lounge, apparently reassured that Paige and Alec were still a couple, Paige asked in a concerned tone, "Did you manage to get any sleep?"

"I think I drifted off about two or three." Pulling his wristwatch from his robe pocket, Alec screeched, "It's only six o'clock!"

Paige smoothed out his unruly hair. "We'd better clear out of here. In minutes, this place will be like Grand Central Station. Most of the officers are out and about when you're still in dreamland."

Not wanting to be seen in his tatty flannel bathrobe, Alec stood up and collected the notes he had written in the dead of night. Together, they walked back to the cabin to get ready for the day.

From a window on the Lido Deck, Alec watched the passengers scurry to the water taxis that were waiting to take them to Philipsburg. They all seemed sure of their destinations. Last evening, Alec believed he knew the killer's identity. But now in the light of day, he wondered whether he was making the pieces fit. Since it was just 7:00 Atlantic Time and 6:00 Eastern Standard Time in Florida, Alec held off phoning McGill. He suspected that the detective wouldn't appreciate a wake up call.

While Alec toyed with his pancakes in the restaurant, he realized he needed to speak with an unbiased individual, someone who could examine the facts impartially and tell him whether he was off base. Pleased to see that person walking toward him, Alec stood up to pull out her chair.

Regina took the offered seat. "What are you doing up so bright and early?"

"You too?"

"You too, what?"

"Oh everyone thinks I sleep too late. I'll have you know, I only had three hours of shuteye last night!"

Regina scrutinized Alec's face. "You've cracked the case, haven't you? I want to hear everything. Don't move. I have to get some herbal tea and a corn muffin, or I won't be able to concentrate."

As she walked away, Alec looked around the dining area. Feeling that their table did not afford enough privacy, he transferred to one that was against a solid wall. At this stage of the game, he didn't want to be over-heard.

Regina returned shortly and had no trouble spotting Alec. While she put down her tray and took her seat, she whispered, "This is a much better location. Now tell me. Who do you suspect, and what made you come to that conclusion?"

After hearing her pose her question so logically, Alec began to sort out his ideas. He told Regina that he felt that the murders were actually reversed and that Mark Linley was bludgeoned because he had seen who put the poisoned suntan oil in Gwen's tote bag. Alec surmised that Linley said or did something the day before his death to alarm Gwen's killer.

Listening keenly up to this point, Regina interjected, "So, you believe it was someone who attended his last meal?"

"How did you know about that?" uttered Alec in amazement.

"Oh, Douglas told me about it. But stop dilly dallying, and tell me who murdered Mark and Gwen."

Alec leaned very close to Regina. "I think it was Janet Kane."

Just as Regina started to say, "But she hardly kn..." she stopped. "You're very clever, Alec. I keep falling into the same trap. She didn't have dislike him or even know him to find him a threat. She merely had to get rid of him."

Getting to the crux of the matter, Regina continued. "What did the controller say at dinner that could have been construed as threatening?"

"Well, when Mark Linley left the table, everyone but Janet said he mumbled the word 'bottle.' Originally, I thought he was referring to Rick

Tanner's DWI charge or the assistant controller's theft of champagne. Now I believe Mark was talking about Gwen's bottle of suntan oil.

"Linley also made a strange remark about Janet's handbag. He told her that it looked very familiar and asked if she purchased it on one of the islands. I think he saw it earlier that day. I strongly doubt he was aware of the significance. But it was enough to frighten Janet."

Regina sipped her tea. "What else do you have? That isn't enough."

Alec shook his head sadly. "Not much. Widarta saw her leave Rick's cabin at 5:00 A.M. to run on the Sun Deck. It would have been easy for Janet to follow Linley to the spa gym, conk him on the head, and then exercise. That afternoon, the women's toilet near the Constellation Lounge needed to be fixed. Janet may have disposed of the bloody wipes in that bathroom as it's on the way to the running track. Since the kid's clubhouse is also on the Sun Deck, I had assumed the towelettes were used to simply clean a baby's bottom."

"Alec, you need physical proof, and I don't mean baby wipes." As Regina said those words, he noticed that she turned her diamond wedding ring so that the stone was centered upright on her finger.

Curious, he asked, "Why do you always fiddle with your ring?"

Glimpsing down at her hands, she replied, "Oh, I think my fingers are shrinking from old age. The diamond keeps moving toward my pinkie. I must get the band resized by a jeweler. At times, it's really uncomfortable."

Regina looked at Alec as if to say, "Why are you asking me that?" On seeing an expression of elation spread across Alec's face, she said aloud, "I've hit upon something important, haven't I?"

Alec grinned. "Yes, you have."

"Well, are you going to tell me what I said?"

Instead Alec got up from his table, kissed Regina's wrinkled, soft cheek, and whispered, "I have an important call to make. If this pans out, I think McGill will have enough probable cause to obtain a search warrant."

Alec took a seat in the infirmary waiting area. Beth told him that the doctor was stitching up a cut, but would be free soon. Alec didn't mind waiting. It gave him a chance to go over his morning thus far.

After leaving Regina, Alec returned to his cabin to phone McGill at home. He caught him just as he was ready to leave for work. The detective found Alec's theories compelling and by the end of their conversation, he promised that he and McHale would track down Janet's jeweler. Alec expected he would be on tenterhooks all day, waiting for McGill to call back.

While Alec was wondering how Douglas would react to the latest turn of events, Beth sat down beside him. Meekly, she inquired, "How are you doing?"

Alec didn't want to appear discourteous, so he gave her his somewhat divided attention, and responded, "I'm fine, lass. What about yourself?"

When she started to tell him about her mother's diabetes, he realized it would be a good time to question her. Interrupting her narration, Alec asked, "Did you happen to see Janet's diamond ring again? She showed it to me several days ago, and I noticed that one of the prong's holding the stone was a bit diff...."

Before he could finish his thought, Beth replied. "I bet that happened when she hurt her finger."

"When did that occur?"

"Oh, it was the day that the controller died."

Barely containing his excitement, Alec probed further. "Do you know how she injured herself?"

"She didn't say. Janet came in that morning, took a handful of band-aids by the front door, and rushed out before I could greet her. I wanted to see her ring again. I was thinking of buying an imitation like it from QVC or HSN."

Alec shook his head in agreement even though he had no idea what a QVC was. "How did you find out the bandages were for her finger?"

"She came back Monday morning when we docked in Florida to say good-bye to the doctor. When Dr. Abbot clasped her hand, I noticed she flinched. Ms. Kane didn't have her ring on, and there were lots of band-aids wrapped around her finger. She must have done a real number on it!"

Alec winked at Beth, rose from the chair, and walked toward the door.

Perplexed, Beth called after him. "Where are you going? You haven't seen the doctor yet!"

Grinning, Alec answered, "Who needs him when I have you."

As he headed down the corridor, he heard giggling.

Alec returned to his cabin to check on his phone messages. Even though McGill hadn't called, Alec's disappointment didn't last long. After all, Beth gave him a valuable piece of information. It could only mean one thing.

Janet not only damaged her ring, but also cut her finger when she attacked the controller. She hit Linley with a ten-pound weight, not thinking to remove her jewelry. The diamond ring turned toward her palm, a prong bent against the rod of the dumbbell, and a corner of the stone tore into the soft fleshy part of her hand. No other explanation seemed plausible.

Feeling that Mark's murder could now be explained satisfactorily, Alec began to focus his attention on Gwen's death. Realizing it would be foolish to wait for McGill to contact him, Alec decided to have lunch and visit Zack in the gym. Before leaving the room, Alec stuffed Janet Kane's picture into his pocket.

On arriving at the spa, Alec learned that Zack just finished a kick boxing class and was in the middle of cleaning up. When the fitness instructor appeared from seemingly nowhere with wet hair, Alec blurted out, "Where did you come from?"

Zack smiled. "Come along, I'll show you."

Alec followed him past the restrooms and down the corridor to the saunas and steam rooms. He hadn't been in that section of the gym before.

Zack stopped outside the men's locker room and said, "I showered in there." Alec opened the door and saw that the room contained two stalls, a sink, a full-length mirror, and a wall of lockers.

Noting that the door of each locker stood wide open, Alec asked, "Why aren't they used?"

Zack smiled, "I see that you don't exercise much. Most passengers don't bring valuables to a workout, and they prefer to shower in their own cabins."

Alec stepped back into the corridor and took a peek in the adjacent utility closet. Arranged neatly on the shelves were terrycloth towels, liquid soap, toilet paper, and other sundry items.

Trying to visualize the setup, Alec asked, "Where did Gwen keep her sunning supplies?"

Zack pointed to the doorknob. "She usually hung her tote bag right here."

"Why didn't she lock it up or put it inside the closet?"

Zack shrugged his shoulders. Sensing that he was monopolizing his time, Alec got to the point. He pulled out the picture of Janet and handed it to the fitness instructor. "Does she come here often?"

Responding with more enthusiasm, Zack grinned. "Sure, that's Ms. Kane. She works out here almost everyday. She uses the treadmill, the triceps extension machine, the preacher curl bench, the shoulder press machine, and various weights."

For a moment, Alec felt that Zack was speaking a foreign language. Undaunted, Alec continued. "Did you ever see her come back here and use these facilities?"

"No, not when I was on duty."

"What about the controller?"

Zack glanced at his wristwatch. Apologetically he replied, "Look, I need to get out front. Linley used the sauna on 'sea days.' He was a very nervous guy and the dry heat helped him relax."

When Zack left, Alec walked over to the men's sauna. From the doorway, Mark would have had a clear view of Janet taking a bottle of suntan oil from Gwen's tote and exchanging it for one in her bag. It would have been a strange sight, but not particularly sinister. The incident would only take on meaning after it was discovered that Gwen was poisoned. Since Janet had no way of knowing when it would occur, she had to get rid of Linley as soon as the opportunity presented itself.

An announcement on the loudspeaker brought Alec out of rumina-
tions. Hearing "Liaison Officer DunBarton, please report to the Security
Desk," Alec dashed out of the fitness center.

When he rapped on Bauer's door, the security man let him in and signaled him to be quiet with the internal "shush" sign. Jarvis was on the
speakerphone with McGill.

Alec took a seat near the desk just as the detective said, "Are you there,
Alec?"

"I'm here."

"Excellent," continued McGill. "I want to talk to you all at once. Pursuing Mr. DunBarton's suggestion, we've collected some preliminary evidence that your passenger, Janet Kane, killed Mark Linley and Gwen
Llewelyn. Alec, you were correct in assuming that she damaged her ring
when she struck Linley with the barbell. Her jeweler repaired the ring
quickly, but didn't get a chance to clean her wristwatch. We had it examined and our lab technician found microscopic particles of Linley's blood
inside the mechanism.

"Later this morning, we were able to obtain a warrant to search Kane's
premises. So far, we've discovered remnants of nicotine patches in her gar-
bage disposal, as well as suntan oil and nicotine residue in a funnel in her
garage. We're building an airtight case against her.

"I would like Officer Bauer to arrest Ms. Kane when she boards the
ship. From her electronic keycard, I understand that she's currently off-
shore in St. Maarten. It would be safer for everyone to have her confined. I
don't want her hearing about her upcoming arrest through gossip. Is that
understood?"

Bauer responded with a question. "The brig is currently occupied.
Would it be acceptable to lock her in her cabin with a security guard
posted at the door?"

"That would be fine. Any other questions?"

Receiving none, McGill added. "Alec, please keep me posted. I'll be
able to take her off your hands on Friday morning when you dock.
Good-bye for now."

When the connection was severed, the captain walked over to Alec and heartily thanked him. Alec imagined that his relief was considerable. He no longer had to worry that one of his officers, staff, or crew was responsible for two gruesome murders.

Alec tossed and turned, attempting to take an afternoon nap. The murder case had been solved, but he felt incredibly uneasy. The song, "This is It," by Kenny Loggins came to mind. "There's no room to run, No way to hide, No time for wondering why. It's here, The moment is now, about to decide." To Alec, the lyrics emphasized the importance of getting on with his *own* life. But it also forewarned him. Janet Kane would not give up easily.

Her arrest went without a hitch. Bauer's men picked her up as she stepped onto the Pegasus. She was taken to her stateroom and told that the Fort Lauderdale Homicide Department wanted her held for the double murders of Gwen and Mark. Bauer removed her phone and advised Rick of her arrest. Nonetheless, Alec was certain he wouldn't get a wink of sleep until he checked on her. He put on his shoes and headed out the door.

As Alec approached her cabin, his sense of apprehension grew. No one was stationed in the hall. Janet's door was locked, but there was no response to his knocks. Alec shouted for the cabin steward to open her door immediately. When he entered the room, Alec's worst fears were realized. The security guard was lying on the floor with a brand new Sheffield knife protruding from his abdomen. Janet's table was laden with a tea tray, and she was nowhere in sight.

CHAPTER 19

▼

"LOVE IS THE ANSWER"

Words & Music—Todd Rungren

Tuesday Afternoon—7th of February

Alec darted over to the injured security guard while he barked out orders to the terrified cabin steward. "Inform the doctor, there's a medical emergency and a crewmember has sustained a deep knife wound to his abdomen. After that, tell Officer Bauer and Captain Jarvis to come here at once. And please hurry!"

The young man ran from the room as Alec knelt beside the downed officer. Recalling the first-aid training he had received as a Boy Scout in Inverness, Alec left the knife where it was to prevent further blood loss. The guard's skin was cool to the touch and his breathing was erratic. Unsure whether he was in shock, Alec promptly elevated his legs and covered him with a spread from Janet's bed. Over and over, he repeated, "Hang in there. Help is on its way."

Moments later, the doctor bustled in. Seeing Douglas approach, Alec stood up quickly and moved aside, giving him access to the crewmember. Douglas methodically checked the officer's breathing, heart rate, and blood pressure.

Bauer came in the room shortly after Douglas finished taking the man's vital signs. The security chief's facial expression turned to one of horror when he noticed his stabbed coworker on the floor. Overwhelmed, he cried, "Oh God, it's Stephen. What's happened?"

Alec shook his head in disbelief. I arrived just minutes ago. I wanted to make sure that Janet was safely tucked away. When I didn't see anyone outside her cabin, I became alarmed and asked the steward to unlock the door."

While Alec was completing his sentence, Maggie Hart scurried in and headed straight toward the doctor. Douglas glanced up and declared, "I need to get him to the infirmary without delay. Where's the stretcher?"

Maggie indicated that it was in the corridor and started to move furniture out of the way. Moments later, she maneuvered the gurney into the stateroom and positioned it next to the body. Alec and Bauer helped the doctor transfer his patient from the floor to a wooden board and then onto the stretcher. The enormity of the situation struck Alec as the officer was wheeled away.

Alec grimaced as he said to Bauer, "It's all my fault. Janet told me she bought a set of knives in Barbados. I can't believe I forgot to tell you about it. I even carried her bloody packages here!"

"Don't reproach yourself," replied Bauer. "It was my responsibility to secure the area. I took the matter too lightly."

Realizing it would be ridiculous to fight over the blame, Alec said, "Right now, we'd better *find* her and fast. How do you want to work this?"

Bauer took a walkie-talkie from his back pocket and began to alert his security team. Within minutes, six men were assembled in Janet's cabin ready to search for her. The chief of security ordered four of his officers to start on A Deck and advance upward through the ship. Alec, Bauer, and the remaining two guards were to begin their pursuit on the Sun Deck and work downward.

By chance, Alec still had Janet's photo in his pocket and showed it to the security team. As it was passed along, several of them commented that she looked quite harmless. Bauer made it clear that she was extremely dangerous and possibly armed. Since she had purchased a seven-piece knife set, Alec started to search her cabin, hunting for the other knives.

Stuffed into a closet were several large Sterlings' shopping bags. In one, Alec found the carton of blades. After counting the number of knives twice, Alec turned to Bauer and said grimly, "Two are gone. Your guard left here with the eight-inch chef's knife stuck in his gut, and she probably took the five-inch utility knife with her."

With heightened sense of awareness, the first members of the squad departed. Following their instructions, they broke up into pairs to investigate the forward and aft sections of each deck.

Jarvis arrived as Alec and Bauer were preparing to leave with the second team. Before Alec could utter a word, the captain stated, "I know what happened. I was in the infirmary when they brought in Officer Randall. Douglas was able to remove the knife and stop the bleeding. Right now, the guard appears stable."

When he turned to go, he spat, "Get her. She's must be deranged to pull a stunt like this on *my* ship."

Alec and a rather burly security guard were directed to explore the aft section of the Sun Deck. Fortunately, there were no passengers out and about that afternoon. The Pegasus was delayed in St. Maarten over an hour, waiting for a tour bus to return from an outing. Alec expected that the captain was going well over twenty knots to make up for lost time. Between the trade winds and the current speed of the vessel, it was exceptionally blustery on the uppermost deck.

Since the back half of the Sun Deck was used for various sports and activities, such as volleyball, table tennis, and shuffleboard, it was flat and offered very little in the way of hiding places. Although there were two storage rooms against one wall, Alec felt certain that they'd be locked. While the officer with him set out to search the area around the dual smoke stacks in the center of the ship, Alec decided to try his luck. He was able to open one door about an inch before it slammed shut. Curious now, Alec pulled harder until the door sprang open. Standing inside the small room was Janet Kane.

Alec's heart sank when he saw that she wasn't alone. Just inches away from Janet's razor-sharp knife stood Paige. Her mouth was gagged tightly with a silk scarf, and her body was bound by badminton netting. It was a ghoulish sight, and Alec could see that Paige was terrified. He knew he'd never forget the way her eyes pleaded for help.

Janet's voice hissed as she declared, "Don't come any closer or this knife will go through her like butter."

Alec's knees went weak. As he stepped back into the wind, he begged, "Please, don't do anything rash. Let me change places with her."

"No this is much better," snarled Janet. "I want to watch you suffer as I carve up her face." To illustrate her point, she pricked Paige on her upper arm. When the crimson blood began to trickle down her limb, Alec, without thinking, took a step forward.

Janet lifted the knife to Paige's neck, right below her jaw line. "Oh no you don't. Unless, of course, you want her to die."

Her eyes glinted like polished obsidian as she raged on. "You've ruined my life. Why did you keep digging? I planned everything perfectly. Rick was mine and I had his parent's eating out of my hand. I deserved to be treated like a queen, and those pests got in my way. You understand that, don't you?"

At that moment, Alec realized that Janet was quite mad. He smiled reassuringly and spoke calmly. "I think I do. Gwen endangered your future."

"On the New Year's Eve cruise, that tramp told me she was pregnant with Rick's baby. I couldn't take a chance she was lying. Rick's father was very anxious for him to produce offspring. If he had known about Gwen's pregnancy, he might have pressured Rick to marry her."

Alec nodded. "I presume that Mark Linley saw you in the gym when you placed the poisoned suntan oil in Gwen's tote bag. He threatened your rightful place in society too. Am I right?"

"Yes. Yes, you do understand." Janet's face softened as she moved closer to Alec. Her gripe on the handle of the knife loosened somewhat. Deciding it was now or never, Alec lurched forward and reached for the weapon.

Part of his blade sliced through Alec's palm. Despite the pain, he held onto the shaft and managed to push Janet against the closet wall. A rack of tennis and ping-pong balls above her head dislodged, and one by one, they dropped to the floor and rolled out of the closet.

When Janet recovered her balance, she lunged for the door. Alec couldn't stop her. As he tried to grasp the corner of her sleeve, he lost his footing.

Even though Janet had a head start, she didn't go far. When Alec emerged from the storage room, he immediately spotted her about forty feet away, precariously leaning against the outside railing of the ship.

"Stay away or I'll jump," she screamed.

The wind made hearing difficult. Alec stopped and yelled, "Janet, please, don't try it. We're at least twelve stories above sea level."

Suddenly, Janet's attention became diverted. She looked past Alec. He turned to see who was behind him and spotted Bauer coming toward them with two security men at his side. Alec called for them to stay where they were, but his warning was lost in a gust of wind. When he faced Janet again, she was gone.

Alec ran to the railing to scan for her body in the ocean. She never made it that far. Janet landed exactly two decks below on the Riviera Deck. From where he stood, it appeared that her neck was broken. Alec deduced that the wind carried her body against the hull when she dived off the side of the ship.

While Bauer and his men departed for the Riviera Deck, Alec raced to the utility closet to free Paige.

This time when Alec saw Paige trussed up like an American Thanksgiving turkey, he was able to smile. He untied the scarf binding her mouth and used Janet's utility knife to free her arms and legs.

At first, Paige had trouble speaking. After several tries, she asked in a scratchy voice, "Di...Did you get her?"

When Alec told her about Janet, Paige started to cry. He held her in his arms and kissed her hair, fearing that the gag bruised her lips.

Rocking her gently, he whispered, "Please Lass, there's no need to cry. It's over now. I'll not let anyone harm you. I love you, Paige."

She smiled while a tear rolled down her cheek.

"From now on, you'll be hearing it a lot more," he added solemnly. "You're my world."

Douglas seated Alec and Paige in his inner office after they were given first aid. The cut on Paige's arm and Alec's palm had been cleansed and bandaged, and Paige was ordered to use a medicated cream on the chafed skin around her mouth. The couple also received inoculations to ward off infection and tetanus.

The doctor, however, was more concerned about Paige's psyche. He was hesitant to give her a strong sedative.

When Douglas pulled out an old bottle of Courvoisier V.S.O.P. from his locked desk drawer, Alec cried, "You old dog. How long have you been hiding that?"

The doctor poured out a large measure of brandy in a plastic cup and handed it to Paige. "It's only for special patients."

Alec snapped, "I want some too."

Paige smiled over her glass. "You'd better give him a drink. He has definitely earned it!"

Once they all had one, Douglas gently said to Paige, "I'd like you to *tell* us what happened. I think it's the best way to treat emotional trauma."

Alec was glad that the doctor broached the subject. He didn't want to exacerbate the situation, but he agreed with Douglas. It would be healthier for Paige to talk about it.

Between sips of cognac, she began to explain. "Janet came by the cruise desk at about three thirty and asked me if I could join her for a walk."

Paige stopped a moment and gazed at Alec. "I knew you suspected her of killing Mark and Gwen, but I didn't want my behavior to make her suspicious. I stupidly agreed to go with her."

Not wanting her to feel responsible, Alec interjected, "Lass, it wasn't your fault. How could you know that Janet was arrested and escaped at knifepoint? I should have stopped off to see you after Bauer locked her up. Instead, I tried to take a bloody nap!"

Paige took Alec's hand and said resolutely, "I think we were both caught up in something much bigger than ourselves."

Sounding calmer, Paige continued. "She wanted to get some fresh air on the Sun Deck even though it was quite windy. At first everything was fine. We talked about my duties on the ship, and she said she wanted to work with Rick after they married.

"Then she asked about our relationship and her manner changed dramatically. She went cr…"

Seeing how hard it was for Paige, Alec asked, "Do you want to stop now? We can try this later."

Paige took a tissue from a box on the doctor's desk and blew her noise. "No, I want to tell you."

After a few moments, she resumed. "Janet became really angry and screamed that *you* ruined her life. She said she had nothing to lose and pushed me into the closet. Then, I noticed she had a knife. I don't know where it came from or whether to fight her off. I was so scared. She promised she wouldn't hurt me if I cooperated."

Alec was very thankful that she complied with her wishes. There was no telling what Janet could have done to Paige if she had struggled with her. Janet easily disabled a strapping young security officer when he merely brought in her tea.

"There's not much more to tell you. She tied me up and told me to stand still. I don't think Janet had it planned out completely. It seemed as though she wanted to hurt as many people as possible before killing herself. Thank God, you came minutes later." Paige added with a smile, "And rescued me!"

Alec and Paige spent their evening quietly. After having a light supper in their cabin, he made Paige get into bed right away. When she appeared to be nodding off, Alec phoned McGill.

The detective admitted that he was disappointed that Janet wouldn't have her day in court, but acknowledged that a good lawyer could have dragged out the case for years over jurisdiction. Eager to get back to Paige, Alec promised to e-mail him in the morning with all the particulars.

When Alec hung up, Paige asked in a sleepy voice, "Is everything okay?"

Alec walked over to her and kissed her cheek tenderly. Finally at peace with the world, he replied, "Things have never been better. I'm just so grateful that we've found each other and you're safe."

As Alec prepared for bed, he acknowledged that his life had taken incredible twists and turn—ones he would *not* have chosen for himself. Yet with all the pain and emptiness he'd experienced in the last six months, he felt that an all-seeing power was directing him to be in the right place, at the right time. Realizing that he had begun to place his trust in that force, Alec sang softly.

> Name your price
> A ticket to paradise
> I can't stay here any more
> And I've looked high and low
> I've been from shore to shore to shore
> If there's a short cut I'd have found it
> Light of the world, shine on me
> Love is the answer

Deciding, he was becoming profound in his old age, Alec got into bed and promptly fell asleep.

EPILOGUE

▼

Friday Afternoon
10th of February
5:20 P.M. EST

The sail-away festivities from Fort Lauderdale were particularly jubilant on Alec's third cruise to the Southern Caribbean. At a poolside table, Alec gazed at the smiling faces of Douglas, Regina, and of course Paige, and made a toast. "Thank you my dear friends for helping me solve my *first* murder case and for patching up my wounds—emotional and physical. To your health and many more adventures on the Pegasus."

Regina lifted her glass and said, "To my new boss, *The Singing Sleuth*!"

Alec grinned and remarked. "I like that nickname. Since I'm no longer the Liaison Officer of this esteemed vessel, you should all call me that."

Paige patted Alec on the knee condescendingly. "The title of Controller suits me fine."

"And how long will we be blessed by your presence?" Douglas inquired.

Alec smiled at Paige and replied, "I've signed up for eight months. My contract ends in October. That's certainly long enough for all of you to hear my full repertoire of songs."

"Oh, Lord," exclaimed the doctor good-naturedly. "I don't think I'll be able to stand the excitement."

Speaking of excitement," uttered Regina, "I saw our chief of security in the jewelry boutique yesterday. He was purchasing a pair of pearl-drop earrings for Miss Van Dam."

Curious, Paige asked, "What did he say to you?"

"He wanted to know what a *woman* thought of them. After I told him they were exquisite, he seemed reassured and thanked me. I have a feeling he and Michelle will be tying the knot one of these days. I've never seen Bauer so blissful."

Douglas grinned ear to ear. "I know another happy couple. Nora told me that she's expecting sometime in August. She didn't want anyone to know she was pregnant until the end of this month. However, I caught her red-handed, thumbing through a book of baby names. After I confronted her, she remarked that she liked the name Alec for a boy and Alecza for a girl. Hmm, Alec. You don't know anything about that, do you?"

"Me?" feigned the controller in a surprised tone. "I just hope that Jeffrey will be a good father and a faithful husband. There will be another murder aboard this vessel if he doesn't behave."

Douglas smiled briefly and then his expression turned somber. "Janet's body was taken away early this morning. I still can't understand what motivated her to murder two innocent people. Thank goodness, the security officer is recovering nicely."

Responding to the doctor's first comment, Regina declared, "I know you were fond of Ms. Kane, dear. But, I'm afraid that I've met people like her before. She was probably deeply scared as a child and grew up with a skewed perception of the world."

Alec added, "Her other half left here a few hours ago. Rick told me he was taking two months off and joining the Capricornus in Copenhagen this April. He was quite civil to me and actually patted me on the back. I guess I saved him from a fate worse than death."

Almost on cue, the new cruise director stood up and presented her able-bodied staff to the passengers. "Oh, look who it is," cried Paige. "I'm so relieved they gave the job to Faith. She's much nicer than that snake who brought Janet among us."

Alec took Paige's hand and squeezed it lovingly. He knew it would take her a while to put the episode behind her. She often woke up in the middle of the night crying and screaming for help.

Over their second round of drinks, Alec and his companions talked about McGill and his closing interviews. The detective boarded the Pegasus at nine that morning to conduct a final wrap up. Even though Boyd was told that Janet Kane committed both murders and died in attempting to escape, McGill wanted to have a word with him.

The detective returned Boyd's engagement ring and let him know that Gwen's body was being shipped to her parents in Wales. Right after their meeting, Boyd left for the airport to catch a plane to Canada. Alec sincerely hoped he'd be able to find closure now that Gwen's killer was dead.

McGill then questioned Douglas about Janet's injuries. The doctor reported that she broke her neck in the fall from the Sun Deck and death occurred instantly. Although the murder inquiry was basically over, McGill promised to e-mail Alec the results of the autopsy once it was completed.

Bauer was seen next. He gave a succinct report about arresting Janet, conducting the search, and recovering her corpse.

Paige followed, and McGill handled her gingerly. He seemed to be exceedingly aware of her emotional state. After Paige signed an affidavit, she appeared much calmer to Alec. It was as if the horror had been transferred from her to an authority figure who was better equipped to deal with the violence.

Alec was with the detective the longest period of time and described the events that led up to Janet's death. He told McGill how Janet reacted and what she said when he discovered her in the sporting goods closet with Paige. To Alec it was rather pointless, but he supposed that McGill liked to have all his *I*'s dotted and his *T*'s crossed.

Once Alec's statement was notarized, he and McGill visited the injured security guard in the infirmary. Officer Randall was resting in bed, awaiting transfer to a hospital in Fort Lauderdale where he would remain for several days.

The young man confirmed Alec's assumptions. Janet asked him to order her some tea and scones from room service. When he carried in the tray and placed it on her coffee table, he briefly saw the glint of the knife as it approached him. With his hands full, he had little opportunity to deflect it.

Once Alec finished enlightening the others, he sighed, realizing that his great adventure was over.

Paige asked, "Are you blue that your sleuthing skills are no longer needed?"

"No, not at all," Alec replied halfheartedly.

Paige smiled at Douglas. "Should I tell him and Regina about our last twenty-one day repositioning cruise to Alaska?"

The doctor winked in response while Alec demanded, "Now Paige, stop teasing! Tell us all about it."

"Well," she remarked with a sly laugh, "We sailed from Port Everglades at the end of April. The Pegasus first stopped at Coral Cay, then Aruba, transited through the Panama Canal, and headed up the West Coast. It wasn't until we had reached Alaska that Officer Bauer discovered a gold Columbian artifact in a hollowed out compartment in the ship's hull. We found out later that it was worth well over a half a million dollars!"

Alec's eyes sparkled. "Now that sounds like my kind of trip. Did you ever find out who placed it there?"

"No. It still remains a mystery. But the statue was returned to the Museo Del Oro in Bogota, Columbia a few months later."

Feeling more upbeat, Alec grinned and said, "I think it's time to eat."

Paige looked at Douglas and Regina with an amused expression. "What am I going to do with him? He's always thinking of his stomach."

As Alec led his flock into the Lido Restaurant for dinner, he whispered to Paige, "I've been known to have a brilliant idea from time to time."

COPYRIGHT ACKNOWLEDGEMENTS

"Live To Tell"
Madonna Ciccone and Pat Leonard
Copyright 1986 WB Music Corp., Bleu Disque Music Co. Inc., Webo
Girl Publishing, Inc., & Johnny Yuma Music
All rights on behalf of Bleu Disque Co., Inc. & Webo Girl Publishing,
Inc.
Administered by WB Music Corp.
All rights reserved. Used by permission.
Page 120

"Love Is the Answer"
Todd Rundgren
Copyright 1977 Warner-Tamberlane Publishing Corp.
Earmark Music Inc. & Humanoid Music
All rights administered by Warner-Tamberlane Publishing Corp.
Alfred Publishing Co., Inc., Miami, FL 33014
All rights reserved. Used by permission.
Page 183

"New York Minute"
Danny Kortchmar, Don Henley, and Jai Winding
Copyright 1989 Woody Creek Music, WB Music Corp,
& Dobbs Music, Inc.
All rights on behalf of Woody Creek Music
Administered by Warner-Tamerlane Publishing Corp.
All rights on behalf of Dobbs Music, Inc.
Administered by WB Music Corp.
Alfred Publishing Co., Inc., Miami, FL 33014
All rights reserved. Used by permission.
Page 98

"One Way or Another"
Deborah Harry and Nigel Harrison
Copyright 1978 Chrysalis Music & Monster Island Music

Page 23

"She's Not There"
Rod Argent
Copyright 1964 Marquis Music Co. Ltd. (PRS)
Administered in USA by Parker Music (BMI)
Courtesy of Fantasy, Inc.
Page 156

"Sweet Talkin' Guy"
Doug Morris, Elliot Greenberg, Barbara Baer, and Robert Schwartz
Copyright 1966 (Renewed 1994) Screen Gems-EMI Music Inc.
& Roznique Music Inc.
Page 70

"They Can't Take That Away From Me"
George Gershwin and Ira Gershwin
Copyright 1936 (Renewed) George Gershwin Music
& Ira Gershwin Music
Page 61

"Things Are Looking Up"
George Gershwin and Ira Gershwin
Copyright 1937 (Renewed) George Gershwin Music
& Ira Gershwin Music

Alfred Publishing Co., Inc., Miami, FL 33014
All rights reserved. Used by permission.
Page 34

"This Is It"
Kenny Loggins and Michael McDonald
Copyright 1979 (Renewed) Milk Money Music
& Tauripin Tunes
Alfred Publishing Co., Inc., Miami, FL 33014
All rights reserved. Used by permission.
Page 175

"Touch Me in the Morning"
Ronald Miller and Michael Masser
Copyright 1972, 1974, 1975, (Renewed 2000, 2002, 2003) Jobete Music
Co., Inc. & Stone Diamond Music Corp.
All rights controlled and administered by EMI April Music Inc. & EMI
Blackwood Music Inc.
All rights reserved. International copyright secured. Used by permission.
Page 47

"You're The Top"
Cole Porter
Copyright 1934 (Renewed) WB Music Corp.
Alfred Publishing Co., Inc., Miami, FL 33014
All rights reserved. Used by permission.
Page 126

"Wedding Bell Blues"
Laura Nyro
Copyright 1966, 1976 (renewed 1994, 2004) EMI Blackwood Music Inc.
All rights reserved. International copyright secured. Used by permission.
Page 147

978-0-595-35452-8
0-595-35452-1

Printed in the United States
39418LVS00005B/103-117